I0535425

PATH UNVEILED

By

KARL HARGESTAM

Original and modified cover art by JelleS and CoverDesignStudio.com

Copyright: Joshua Media & Publication Corp. ISBN: 978-0-9893220-3-4

JOSHUACAMPAIGN
I N T E R N A T I O N A L

JOSHUA MEDIA & PUBLICATION CORP.

Box 8700, Fresno, CA 93747, USA

Toll Free (800) 745 1332, Fax (866) 888 0572
email: JCI@joshuacampaign.com

www.joshuacampaign.com

www.missionsoneeleven.com

www.theassignmentshow.tv

"And now remains faith, hope, charity, these three; but the greatest of these is charity"

1 Cor. 13:13

CHAPTER 1: Haiti

The pile of amputated limbs lay lumped together outside a medical tent that a slight breeze with an annoying rhythm caused to make a flapping sound. Regardless of type and depending on its freshness, blood of various shades of red mingled among shards of flesh as various ligaments clung to each other, stuck as though searching for a natural reattachment that wasn't forthcoming.

At the end of the day workers shoveled the pile of flesh into wheelbarrows, pushing the load to an open pit near the edge of the encampment where an eternal bonfire sent the smell of burnt bone into the air.

It'd been weeks since the devastating earthquake had shaken the foundations of Haiti, and it's capital Port-au-Prince, leaving thousands of dead in its wake and planting a quarter million corpses into the earth and sending hundreds of thousands more trembling under the cover of uncertainty. While teams of aid workers rushed to tackle the disaster knowing it'd be months if not years before the place picked itself back up. However 'normal' might be defined in Haiti, it still rated as abnormal compared to everywhere else. This side of the island was a broken

3

country even before the quake and now it was smacked even further down by what seemed like the wrath of god.

A thinning Dr. Yossi Peer, his hair graying at the peripheral by the day, exited the medical tent and glimpsed the pile of limps. Situated atop the mangled flesh, was the little girl's leg he'd amputated less than a half-hour earlier. The procedure had been to no avail. He'd declared the girl dead only moments ago.

He wiped the sweat from his brow. The tropical sun only added to his misery. Sweat, blood, tears that was Haiti. Graft and corruption had robbed Haiti's people of even the basic medical supplies for decades. Now when the demand for medicines was at a premium, there was none to be found. From simple abrasions to deep wounds, the injuries people suffered during the seismic trauma were routinely becoming infected, leaving amputation as the only cure.

The only immunity people seemed to possess was to any aversion at the sight of thousands roaming Port-au-Prince missing a limb. While many survived such procedures, Dr. Yossi Peer witnessed firsthand there was just as many who succumbed to their injuries. The little girl, whose body he watched a laborer load onto a cart, was the latest mortality statistic, a notation in the paperwork to be turned in later.

"Come on, Doc. I will drive you back to the compound," a driver said.

Riding through the capital back to the compound was never a sure-thing. Yossi was accompanied by a driver and a guard, who while he kept his weapon out of sight, was armed none of the less for a firefight. Well-armed gangs ruled most neighborhoods. They controlled the markets, instigating fear into residents and strangers alike. There was no army or police to speak of capable of intervening. Haiti was a place of survival by any means imaginable.

The driver zigzagged through traffic often creating his own lane while following the path of least resistance. Colorful top-tops, converted pickups that served as local buses were decorated with religious slogans designed to entice divine protection and profit. All prayers were solicited and no religion was exempt. The top-top art was also good business. The more decorative the vehicle, the more passengers it attracted. A good driver kept his vehicle looking fresh and changed the designs regularly.

Clusters of debris monumentalized the earthquake's devastation. Merchants were back in business selling what they could to eke out a net profit of a few dollars a month. Yossi knew most of the wares sold were flowing through black marketeers. Many of the goods had actually been looted from aid shipments. Nongovernmental organizations (NGO) were discovering that graft was an essential component in Haiti's social fabric.

As they drove by it, Yossi glanced at the Presidential palace lying in ruins. For decades the prime residence of the Duvalier family who under the auspices of their absolute powers had plundered the country's treasury at will, the palace's roof had collapsed. The structure had crumbled as though squeezed by the hand of Justice during the earth's shaking.

Across the street from the palace, scavengers picked through a garbage dump looking for enough scraps to make a meal. A kid, Yossi guessed maybe nine or 10, held a makeshift rope acting as a leash tied around his pet cat. One hand was on the leash, and the other was on a stick used to poke and shift through the garbage for anything salvageable. In the perfect world, the boy would've been playing with the little girl Yossi had lost back in the operating tent but it wasn't a perfect world, or even a just one, and the most Yossi hoped for at this point was that the cat survived the night.

Yossi had mistakenly thought his last assignment in Ethiopia was tough. He wouldn't have left except the aid agency had put out an S.O.S. for any doctor or nurse wishing to volunteer for a couple of months to pick up stakes and wing it to Haiti.

Yossi calculated he might make a difference when he agreed to rush to Port-au-Prince. But now, all the skills learned in medical school, the emergency room, or even the harsh reality of Africa, seemed inadequate for the tide of suffering in this tropical catastrophe.

Their vehicle turned onto a road running up the side of a mountain whose landscaped had been stripped of vegetation long before the quake occurred. Yossi noted a sacrificed chicken limp in the roadway. Its neck had been wrung and the blood drained in a voodoo ritual the night before. These days, while churches continued to hold the survivors in their congregations together by meeting in crumbling buildings or beneath sheltering tarps, the locals weren't afraid to hedge their bets by offering up a price intended to invoke other supernatural forces. Voodoo had always rivaled Christianity in Haiti and though Christian roots ran deep, the superstitions of the local ancestors hadn't been eradicated.

Entering the compound, a massive camp of tents ran right until butting the building lodging the aid staff. The building also doubled as an unofficial office. The setup was as chaotic as the crisis itself.

The earlier image of the girl dying on the table stuck in his mind. He had taken the leg to save her life; instead complications claimed her as though destiny was collecting a debt. He didn't even think she had a family to mourn for her. It was as though she never existed.

"Is this as good as it gets?" Yossi asked himself afraid to probe his soul for an answer.

He paused at the entrance to the place that was his temporary home. The stench of rotting corpses carried in the wind irritating his nostrils until his face turned up.

Nearby, collapsed buildings stood out in the setting sun. Victims lay in those ruins. They'd never been recovered and now in the tropical heat the whiff of mortality reminded Yossi that the worse was still to come.

"Slightly on the putrid side today, isn't it?" Dr. Jonas Johns commented. Chief of Surgery at one of the largest hospitals in Baltimore, he'd been assigned to oversee medical operations immediately after the quake. He was anxious himself to be relieved in a couple of weeks and go back to the more familiar confines of Baltimore, his two daughters, and a wife he was sure was redecorating the house to her specifications in his absence.

'Slightly," Yossi replied.

"You look a little ... how was your day?" Jonas asked.

"Lost another one," Yossi wondered how much harder his heart had to become in order to deflect the pain of saying those words.

"Amputation?"

Yossi nodded, "Little girl, couldn't have been more than nine or 10."

"We're seeing more of that these days and I suppose it won't subside any time soon," Jonas noted.

"Suppose not."

Jonas could see Yossi's thread of composure was unraveling ever so slightly. "They just turned on the generator. Why don't you catch a shower before dinner?"

In the shower, Yossi let the water run over his body. Despite being soaked down, he felt no cleaner. Dust, decay and death clung to his spirit strangling the very faith that'd led him into this type of work. He'd lost people before, close people, but if he couldn't save a little girl then what were his talents worth? Why was he continuing to work in specks on the map that were the frontier of the abyss? One couldn't close an abyss only avoid falling into it.

This abyss was swallowing him whole. While his instinct was to fight on, Yossi simultaneously experienced fear. The joy of his work was consumed by the burning embers of destruction he walked across every morning. A heart could only simmer for so long before it passionately burst into flames or imploded under its own weight.

Yossi wasn't aware that he'd slid to the floor of the shower until Jonas' interruption pulled him into the present moment.

"Sorry, partner. I didn't realize … you're using a lot of water up here so I came up to check on you. Then I heard the sobbing and well …"

Yossi picked himself up off the shower floor, aware of tears in his eyes for the first time. A sniffle indicated he'd been on the floor longer than he thought.

"It's ok. Yes, you're right. Sorry, I must have lost track of time."

"Why don't you finish up, get dressed, and see me in my office before we eat. Say five minutes? That sound, ok?" Jonas gently insisted.

"Yeah, sure. I'll be right down," Yossi grudgingly agreed.

In the little room that pre-quake served as someone's ideal of a den, Jonas maintained an office consisting of a folding table improvising as a desk and folding chairs that'd been rescued from a destroyed school and resold on the black market.

"Have a seat," Jonas invited. Yossi was busy sizing up a tall redheaded man with the makings of a scruffy beard slouched in one of the chairs. The man had his elbow propped up on Jonas' desk.

"Yossi, this is Colonel David Landsberg. He's with the IDF medical unit across town."

"Hello," Yossi said.

"Likewise, I'm sure," the man replied as though not paying attention at all.

"Don't worry. David knows how to be, shall we say confidential?" Jonas assured Yossi.

"Oh, I'm very confidential. Mainly, because I have enough secrets of my own, I don't need to worry about anyone else's," David stated.

"You're a doctor with the IDF?" Yossi asked.

"The rank belongs to the IDF, a leftover from reserve duty."

"And the doctor part?" Yossi probed.

"To tell the truth, I can't tell a scalpel from a kitchen knife. I'm a lawyer with the IDF, at least on this mission," David explained.

"David is the legal liaison between the IDF team and the Haitians. I wish we had a liaison," Jonas commented wistfully.

Yossi concurred, "It would be handy."

"We use to date the same girls back in college, didn't we?" Jonas recalled fondly.

"No, I use to give you the ones I didn't want to date. How do you think so many girls got your number?" David joked.

"And here, I thought they were holding out for a man with potential," Jonas quipped.

"Yeah, who figured college girls could prove so shallow, right?"

"About upstairs …" Jonas started.

"Sorry, about that. It won't happen again," Yossi assured Jonas almost sounding military-like himself.

"But it's happened before, right?" Jonas inquired but all he got in reply was a telling silence from Yossi.

Jonas went on, "Listen, places like this, they'll always exist. Unfortunately, like today, we lose as many as we save. Sometimes, we lose more. I can't explain why the world is the way it is. Maybe someday it will change but that someday is a long way off. We all know that."

"Yeah, I know it. Don't worry, I'm fine," Yossi assured Jonas.

"I saw your version of fine upstairs," Jonas replied.

"I told you that I'm fine. Chalk it up as just a bad day," Yossi stressed with more force in his voice.

Jonas softened his tone, "I'd be derelict in my duty if I didn't make sure you were all right. We care about you, Yossi. I care about you. You're a fine doctor, one of the best. The group here is lucky to have you. I just want to make sure the environment here doesn't gain the upper hand. We all need a little release from time to time. If we didn't, we'd all go insane in a place like this."

Yossi squirmed at having been caught in such a vulnerable position.

"There's no shame in it," Jonas assured him. It was a curse of the profession that they were expected to deal with death without strain on their own emotions.

"I promise you, I am fine," Yossi declared with more bluntness than he intended.

"Well that is my call to make not yours," Jonas pointed out.

David interrupted, "You know, there is a position …"

Yossi curtly cut him off, "Excuse, me, but this is really none of the IDF's business and certainly not yours."

"Well, let's say it is, just for the time being," David shot back.

Yossi was taken back. "Excuse me?"

"Not yet. As I was saying, there is a post for a man like you in Tel Aviv. Well, Holon to be exact. I told Jonas here,

I can arrange an assignment to the Wolffsohn Hospital there on a short-term basis. It will be a good change of pace for you and as far as I can tell from your file, and from what Jonas has told me, you'd be a fine addition to the team," David explained.

Yossi looked straight into Jonas' eyes, "I can't leave. You need me."

"No man is irreplaceable. The misery in this country is going to be around for a long time to come. What I do know is that the world benefits not one iota if I send a doctor, I remind you a competent one; back into it that is spiritually broken after leaving here.

Look, we all reach that brink. I worked the Indonesian tsunami and had nightmares for weeks afterward. I couldn't go to a beach for six months and I love the beach."

" Look …" Yossi started.

"My mind is made up," Jonas declared.

"Just like that?"

"No, but that is the decision and I can assure you it is final," Jonas informed him.

David interjected, "You'll fit in with the team in Tel Aviv just fine."

"Do I have a choice?" Yossi asked.

"From what Jonas is saying, my impression is no, you don't."

"I'll make sure all the paperwork is cleared with our umbrella group, Global Missions Group so you'll lose none of your standing with them," Jonas promised.

Yossi resisted the temptation to burn a bridge. "I appreciate that."

"Do you have someone to talk to?" Jonas asked as Yossi rose from his chair.

"Like who?" Yossi shot back with a residue of venom.

"I don't know; a wife? Girlfriend?"

"No."

"Do you want me to call one of the missionaries and have them stop by?" Jonas offered.

"To counsel me? No, I don't think so. And I suppose you want me to see a rabbi?"

David smirked, "No, you're a goy. What good would a rabbi do?"

"Take the break. Enjoy the pleasures of Israel. The sunshine. The beach. I hear they have great beaches," Jonas said.

"Some of the best," David confirmed.

Yossi reached for the door knob.

"If you had someone to unload on, maybe it would help. Maybe you should work on finding a girlfriend or even a wife," Jonas suggested.

"You're married. Do you tell your wife about all this?" Yossi asked.

"Not a chance," Jonas replied.

"And what does this team do in Tel Aviv?" Yossi sarcastically asked.

"Transplant organs for orphans from around the world. I thought you might like to work with injecting a little hope into the world for a few months. Any objections?" David asked.

"Do I have a choice?" Yossi speculated aloud.

"From what Jonas, says, no," David answered.

CHAPTER 2: Love At Last Sight

Cole Tarkington threw up his hands in disgust, and failing to gain satisfaction from that fruitless gesture, slapped the steering wheel of his fire engine red Jeep Cherokee three times in rapid succession to vent his emotion. His fingers gripped the steering wheel in an act of substitute strangulation worthy of the Boston Strangler himself. Still, it was a rare performance of road rage for the mild mannered St. Clair, Indiana High School history teacher.

"What's the matter, dad?" Eric questioned from the backseat with a tone of confidence that, if you didn't know he wasn't even a teenager yet, sounded as though he was single-handedly capable of intervening and fixing the source of frustration. As Eric waited patiently for the explanation he held zero expectation of receiving, he tugged at the blue dress jacket and striped tie his mother had forced him to wear that day. The last time he'd been dressed in this outfit was Easter. Since then, he'd secretly plotted in his mind how he might make it disappear from his closet without his mother knowing. He was anxious to get home and throw his Levi's back on.

"What is wrong with you today?" Monique demanded of her husband, keeping her voice lowered out of embarrassment even though the three of them were the only occupants in the car.

She folded up the compact mirror she'd been using to brush the remnants of the rice shower from her hair. The rice had been intended for the bride and groom but the teenagers at the wedding, spying wackiness in the occasion that no one else did, determined everyone should share in the festivities. They'd flung the rice freely among attendees rendering the costly hairdo Monique had obtained the day before much less attractive.

"Would you just drive? At this rate, we'll be the last ones arriving at the reception." Monique's scolding enticed a frustrated *give me a break* look from Cole. Her husband pointed in the direction of his agitation.

"What ...' Monique's started until her eyes latched onto the green Chevy van stopped in front of them. It was the style of van that you would expect to pop up on *That 70's Show* or *The A-Team*. And like those shows, it had long ago outlived its usefulness as emphasized by the patches of peeled paint dotting the vehicle. The oil laced smoke emitting from the tailpipe spoke to the wear and tear the engine had experienced over the decades. The van made the case for why the Environmental Protection Agency had set emissions standards in the first place.

"Do you think Henry Ford imagined a contraption that ugly when he rolled out the Model T? The thing is a rolling fossil. And look! Just look!" Cole exclaimed.

The rear window of the van was peppered by stickers from bands that had, in their short garage based careers, lacked the compelling story of a Johnny Rotten and consequently had long ago been swept into the dustbin of rock and roll wannabes. It was the sticker on the bumper though that triggered Cole's outburst. It simply read, *MOVE IT!*

The traffic light showed green but the van idled away burning fuel at a horrendous rate and holding up the Tarkington's simple trek across town to the Shiner's Hall where the reception was located. The half dozen cars behind them weren't experiencing the love either.

Monique's eyes latched onto the bumper sticker. Without hesitation she reached over and laid on the horn.

"Mo!" Cole cautioned.

She ignored him. Leaning her head out the window, she yelled, "*Move It* yourself, buster!"

Pulling her head back inside she mumbled, "I swear. Some days, I think the world's populated by morons."

19

She saw Cole's astonishment as from the backseat Eric giggled.

"I'll have none of that back there, young man, you hear me?" Monique cautioned with a finger that didn't wag but pointed straight at its target like a missile honed in on its target waiting for someone to punch the right button.

"Babe, don't you think ..." Cole started before Monique cut him off.

"What? What? You're the one slapping the steering wheel. I'm just trying to jump starting things here. We don't have all day you know. They'll be opening the presents at the reception and ours won't even be sitting on the table because we're stuck behind a moron." She laid on the horn again.

"Mo!"

"Ah, look, the light is turning yellow. This idiot is going to make us sit through a whole other light again. Can you believe this?"

Just about the second Monique finished whining; the van lurched forward and ventured through the intersection leaving a haze of exhaust in its trail.

"Go baby, go!" Monique urged.

Cole pushed the gas only to see the light turn red. With the emergence of a red light, Cole's instincts took over. His subconscious had his foot slamming the accelerator to the floor before he even comprehended what he was doing. What he did grasp rather quickly was the siren blaring from the cop car that had turned in pursuit at the intersection.

"Oh, man," Cole muttered. Monique looked behind them as Cole pulled the car toward the shoulder of the road.

"Cool! You going to jail dad?" a clearly excited Eric asked.

"Don't be silly. Your father isn't going to jail." Monique answered in a firm motherly tone.

"You going to lie your way out of it?" Eric quizzed.

"No!" Monique shot back. "Now sit yourself down in the seat and stay quiet."

"Aw, mom!"

"Don't 'aw, mom' me. If you know what is good for you then you'll keep silent."

"Don't be hard on him, Mo," Cole pleaded.

"Thanks, dad," Eric piped in.

"No, problem, son," Cole answered.

Monique's eyes squeezed tighter around the stare she was giving Cole like an Iron Maiden encasing its victim.

Monique's concentration was snapped by a musical chime sounding from the back seat. She turned her gaze in time to see Eric texting a picture of the policeman exiting his

21

vehicle. She grabbed the cellphone and tossed it toward her purse on the floorboard.

"But mom! I was sending that to Jason!"

"At least he wasn't uploading it to YouTube," Cole pointed out.

"Could you help out here a little?" Monique pleaded.

"He's just archiving the moment."

"Tell me, teacher man, when does a kid worry about 'archiving'? Do you actually speak to your students this way? Boy, do I pity them. You know, it's your fault we're in this mess to begin with," Monique griped.

Cole was taken back, "My fault? And leave my students out of this would you?"

"Yes, your fault," Monique reaffirmed.

"My fault? How …" Cole was interrupted by the policeman's tap on the door.

"Yes, officer?" Cole inquired with all the convincing innocence of an altar boy who'd just been caught with a communion wafer in his mouth.

The officer bent over to gain a better view of the inside of the vehicle, and with one hand resting on his holster, asked, "Sir, do you realize you sped through a red light at the intersection back there?"

Before Cole could formulate an explanation, the officer continued, "Sir, let me see your license and registration, please."

The sigh escaping Cole's body was a sign of resignation as he surrendered to the officer's request.

"Do you know how much a ticket is going to add to our insurance?" Monique half-whispered, half-scolded.

"Are you getting a ticket, dad?" Eric asked.

"Keep quiet would you, son?" Cole sounded angrier with Eric than intended.

Monique flashed him a stern look of statutory awareness that speechlessly said, *now you set your foot down with him?*

"Sir, where are you going in such a hurry?" the officer asked.

"My wife and I were just headed to a wedding reception," Cole answered.

"You part of the wedding party?" the officer inquired.

"No but the groom's someone we know from church," Cole explained.

"Then the hurry really isn't worth the ticket I have to give you is it?"

"No, I suppose it isn't."

"He doesn't always think these things through."
Monique's statement was released aimlessly without any
particular recipient in mind although it was cause enough
for the officer to give her a once over.

"You two wait here," the officer ordered.

Cole and Monique slumped against the doors in their
respective corners without even bothering to glance at each
other let alone speak. In the backseat, Eric silently turned
his head from one corner to the next having had rarely
witnessed the two combatants retire from battle quite so
willingly before.

Upon his return, the police officer hesitated briefly,
"It's not really my place to say but you two seem like you
need to take a little break from things. I sense a little
tension here and while none of it involves the criminal
system – *yet* - it's probably not a good sign you're letting
your boy here witness your behavior. You're going to a
wedding reception, right? It might be an opportune time to
remember how your wedding was while there, just to put
things in perspective. Sign here." The officer held out the
ticket on a clipboard as Cole dutifully signed it while
Monique gently tapped her head against the door window.

The remainder of the ride proved pure sharp edged
silence, the kind that slices and dices to the core without

anyone's direction. The whole car ride – this time with Cole purposely driving five miles under the speed limit to avoid a second ticket – would've continued at mortuary levels if it hadn't been for Eric.

"Couldn't you have talked him out of giving you a ticket, dad?"

"Was he trying to say you guys need a vacation? How about Disneyland? Think we could go to Disneyland? Oh, or I know! Six Flags! They have that new rollercoaster that's really cool!"

"How come the van didn't get a ticket? The whole thing was the van's fault wasn't it? I mean mom said the guy was an idiot."

"Do cops get to take their cars home?"

"Do I have to keep wearing this stinking tie?"

"*Yes!*" Both parents shouted in unison.

"Ok, ok. Geez, I was just asking," Eric mumbled.

The Shriner's Hall, where rentals included the folding chairs and tables, had been decorated the night before with a variety of party supplies stocked at the edge of town Wal-Mart Superstore. The groom's side of the family had emptied the store's shelves of party ribbons and picnic supplies.

Festive ribbons designed more for a Fourth of July party spruced up the tables and walls. Sitting on a table all its own, a double layered white-iced wedding cake from the bakery section, with giant red roses trimming the edges, tempted the obligatory finger swiper. The Ken and Barbie of the pastry business, a standard plastic bride and groom, sat lodged atop the cake waiting to be fawned over by googly-eyed hosts and guests.

A distant relative from the groom's side had taken the wrapped toaster – also purchased at Wal-Mart - from the Tarkington's with a well-practiced gracious smile, and set it in a pile on a front table near the cake. A stack of knock-off Hallmark cards were spread out in orderly fashion next to the presents.

"Cole!" Rev. Bill Hasbro shook his hand.

"Monique."

"Reverend," Monique replied putting her hand forth.

"I see you even have the little guy dressed up for the occasion." Rev. Hasbro's pat on the head caused Eric to recoil slightly. He resented people treated him like the family pet.

"Nice crowd out today," Cole noted.

"Yes, yes, it is." Rev. Hasbro glanced around the room rather pleased people had shown their support for the newlyweds.

"I suppose everyone came out for Jimbo," Monique stated.

"I do believe you're right. I don't even know if the bride has any family here beside her mother." Rev. Hasbro motioned toward a middle aged lady dressed in a specially sewn dress configured with the wedding party colors of rose and tan.

"Why'd they have the reception here and not at the Church dining hall?" Cole asked.

"I offered to let them use it but Jimbo is a Shriner and I think they let him have this place as a wedding present," Rev. Hasbro replied.

"I can't believe Jimbo actually married her," Monique half-whispered.

Rev. Hasbro shrugged. He'd known the rumor mill in the church had been busy ever since Jimbo – because of his football size people called him Jimbo as though he'd been born in the swamps of Louisiana instead of the dilapidated row houses of Gary, Indiana - and Mary Ann had started seeing each other. Rev. Hasbro ignored the rumors because in his experience love often literally made strange bedfellows.

"Why not?" Cole asked.

"Well, because …" Monique hesitated for a moment trying to mentally pinpoint a diplomatic way of putting her answer but after a few seconds she quit worrying about the correctness of her reply.

"There's just such an age difference between them. He's nearly 60 and she's like a freshman in high-school."

She knew the age difference wasn't that drastic but the gap was still difficult to ignore. Jimbo was nearing 60 although he looked a good 10 years younger. His receding hairline only made him look distinguished as he managed to stay in shape with his small roofing business. Nothing like hauling shingles up and down the ladder to build the biceps and brides in their late-20s liked well formed biceps.

Mary Ann came off like she'd be more comfortable entering a wet T-shirt contest at spring break than assuming the role of a responsible wife. Monique suspected Jimbo was in over his head with this marriage.

"Don't be harsh," Cole said.

"Sure, a guy would say that," Monique quipped.

Cole defended his position, "I'm just saying I'm happy Jimbo found someone after his ex ran off the way she did. "

Monique conceded the point, "Yeah, I guess you're right. He was depressed for so long."

"You'd be depressed too if your wife ran off with the garbage man on your birthday." Cole shook his head thankful that he hadn't had to worry about such incidents with Monique.

"At least he rooted himself back into church," Rev. Hasbro pointed out, "and his new bride, Mary Ann, is coming every Sunday with him."

"I am glad we didn't have to go through all this, aren't you?" Monique asked.

Cole smiled. "Yeah, I was stressed out enough."

"As I recall, you two could hardly wait to honeymoon," Rev. Hasbro said.

"Yeah, we went to Brown County," Cole explained remembering the cabin they rented away from it all. Of course the cabin did come with a hot tub which they managed to get their money's worth out of.

Monique smiled as Cole flashed her knowing approval. There'd been no reception on their wedding day just a simple ceremony at the church with only a half-dozen people in attendance. Both she and Cole had wished it that way.

Cole preferred the scaled down festivities and for Monique, she had never expected anything more than the French civil ceremony so it was fine. She had worn a new blue dress with gold trimming that spoke of elegance. Cole had yanked out a suit from the back of the closet. Their bags had been packed and were waiting for them when they finished. Instead of a reception, they'd done a clothes-change and road-tripped to the middle of nowhere for a romantic weekend.

Rev. Hasbro was pleased to see the couple enjoy a moment together. Lately, he'd noticed more tension than normal between them. While rough patches were normal in any marriage, he knew from the couples he'd counseled over the years, it wasn't wise to let those tensions linger. After a while, they tended to fester.

"What is Mary Ann really like? I've only talked to her a couple times at church, mainly, to say hello or goodbye," Cole said.

"How'd they meet?" Monique was curious.

"I can't say I rightly know. She seems to cling to Jimbo is all I know. I was happy to do the ceremony for them. I am sure she will become more involved with the congregation as time goes on," Rev. Hasbro replied.

At that moment, Jimbo and Mary Ann entered the room to a round of applause. A photographer snapped their pictures as they gathered themselves behind the head table where the presents were now stacked by size like building blocks.

Mary Ann ran her hand over the packages as the blessed couple feigned surprise at having received anything at all. Suddenly, she flashed a look of disgust at a guest nearby who was engaged in a cell phone discussion about a tee-off time.

"No, I should be there in say an hour. That'd be fine. Go ahead and get the cart too." The man caught a glimpse of Mary Ann's displeasure.

"You know, I need to go. I'm at that thing. Yeah that thing. Talk to you later, ok? Good. See you then." Acting as though it was the normal course of business, the man ended the call and slid the phone back into his pocket.

Mary Ann started opening the cards, pulling a check out of one, but then Jimbo whispered something in her ear. She nodded her agreement, motioning to one of the church ladies who in turn solicited help in carrying the cake over to the table.

It took a little maneuvering to move the presents and make enough room for the cake but it gave the

photographer time to snap presentable shots before it was
devoured.

While the hosts were positioning themselves, Rev.
Hasbro leaned over and asked, "So have you thought about
the trip anymore?"

Cole grimaced at the topic. This was the hundredth time
Rev. Hasbro had brought the subject up and each time the
talk ended with the same result.

"Bill. Come on. You know we've gone over this. You
know I don't feel right taking a trip with the church that
isn't directly missions related. We've had this discussion. If
I am going to spend the money, then I want to be doing
something other than sightseeing."

"I know, I know. But don't think of this as a *trip*.
Consider it more of a pilgrimage. It is the Holy Land after
all; the very place where Jesus walked," Rev. Hasbro
contended.

"I understand that, Bill. But I don't need to see where
Jesus walked to believe in him."

"Of course you don't. I'm not insinuating you do. But
what I am saying is that the trip will reaffirm your faith. It
will not only bring the New Testament but the whole Bible
alive for you. Imagine walking the very streets Jesus
walked?"

"I suspect they've been paved since then. Besides, I really do prefer driving around St. Clair," Cole stated.

"And running red lights," Monique grabbed the free dig.

"What?" a confused Rev. Hasbro asked.

"Ignore her, please," Cole told him.

Rev. Hasbro continued, "Think of all the history though. Jerusalem is called the City of David after all. It'd be right down your alley. Like I said, it's a pilgrimage. You'd be like the crusaders venturing over there to claim the holiest spots for Christianity."

"Hopefully, without the body count they left in their wake. No that Ukraine trip was a pilgrimage. I really don't need another," Cole sarcastically countered. The last minute mission's trip the church had sent Cole on to the Ukraine, on behalf of the Global Missions Group, had been problematic from the moment they purchased the tickets. Monique had originally been tapped to go along but in the end Eric had been bed-ridden with a severe case of the flu so Monique stayed behind to make sure the boy had the attention he expected and deserved.

Rev. Hasbro chuckled slightly. "No one ever said there wouldn't be a few trials along the way."

"A few trials? Ha! Next time you should come along. It will redefine your definition of long-suffering," Cole retorted.

"Jimbo and Mary Ann are coming along on the tour. It's his wedding present to her. Apparently, she's anxious to see the world," Rev. Hasbro noted.

"Well, these days, we just don't have the money for a Holy Land tour anyway," Monique announced.

"Plus, I can't take any time off from my job at the call center. I haven't been there long enough yet to request time off," she added.

"How is the job going?" Rev. Hasbro inquired.

"Humph," Monique responded.

"That bad?"

"Ever hear of a call center this side of Mumbai that was the ideal job?" Monique asked.

"No. I guess not," Rev. Hasbro conceded.

"Well, after closing the business, I had to take what I could get. It wasn't my first choice," Monique explained with a sadness laced voice.

"Oh, look, they're cutting the cake." Cole didn't care if they cut the cake or if he even received a piece with an iced-rose or not. He wanted to divert the conversation to something other than a church tour to the Holy Land or his family's financial woes.

"Jimbo does look happy doesn't he?" Rev. Hasbro noted.

"Wouldn't you be?" Cole chuckled.

"I love her shoes." Monique observed the shiny, unscuffed, slender beige heels the bride was wearing. Everything else in the hall may have been a Wal-Mart purchase but those weren't. She wondered how much the credit card bill had set Jimbo back.

The hall festively gawked as the happy couple cut the cake and took take a slice for themselves. Jimbo juggled the piece in his hand and before anyone could stop it, the piece plopped onto the floor prompting Mary Ann in her wedding dress to hop backwards avoiding the splatter of icing. Sheepishly, Jimbo smiled, shrugging his shoulders as to say *what you going to do?* It wasn't the most embarrassing event in his life but he wasn't going to do a public comparison.

Mary Ann, who'd grown accustomed to Jimbo's clumsiness (after all this was the guy who'd dropped his cellphone into the penguin pen at the zoo on their first date), moved in to save the moment.

She graciously picked up her piece of cake. She reached out to Jimbo who instinctively cocked his head backward to avoid being force fed but then slowly allowed himself to inch inward so that Mary Ann could feed the cake into his mouth.

Jimbo could feel his face becoming a sticky mess. Mary Ann wasn't worried about the appearance. Just the opposite, she found the messy situation comical and began shoving the piece into Jim's mouth. It was a trailer park move but then again, mobile homes were all she'd known until now.

There was a splatter of laughter as people who'd known Jimbo for years feasted on his joyous humiliation. Camera phones captured the moment prompting a YouTube posting later.

For the moment though, it seemed to observers that the day may be passing Jimbo by in a haze for he seemed to not be concentrating on the crowd, the presents, or even his bride as he jerked back from the cake even though Mary Ann still had some left in her hand.

Mary Ann waved the remainder of the piece jokingly under her new husband's nose, "To much, honey? Aw, poor thing."

Mary Ann noticed Jimbo was trying to smile but his mouth was having trouble forming an expression. His eyes were oddly staring at her.

"What's the trouble, baby? Take it down the wrong pipe? You want some punch?" Jimbo was too busy trying to swallow to answer.

Mary Ann turned to a group of guests, "Can you get us some punch, please?"

All she felt after that was Jimbo's body brushing her dress as he crashed face down into the cake sending the plastic Ken and Barbie sliding across the Shriner's Hall floor.

A scream from a church lady echoed between the Shriner's Hall walls before she fainted, falling backward toward the arms of a Sunday school teacher. Unfortunately for the church lady, the Sunday school teacher's first instinct was to step aside, letting her fall into a row of folding chairs.

"Jimbo? Come on, get up Jimbo. People are watching," a shocked Mary Ann pleaded as though Jimbo had somehow tripped over his own two feet.

There was a mad scramble by some of the men to reach Jimbo although the scrum was slowed up by the smashed cake and icing on the floor. It seems no one wanted to stain their Sunday best. Still, when they did reach Jimbo, they flipped him over and cleared his face.

One of the men kept hollering, "Jimbo. Jimbo. Jimbo!'
but it was clear to all present that if Jimbo had been able to
hear, he would've answered the first time around.

"Sister Wilma is out like a light. We need a doctor here,"
the Sunday school teacher shouted.

"Someone should call 911," a nearby lady yelled,
prompting a rash of people to yank out their cell phones.
Later, the St. Clair Police Department released a report on
the incident describing how the sudden influx of calls in the
first minute overloaded the emergency system.

"911 isn't going to do Jimbo any good," a man bent over
Jimbo's body declared.

Hearing this, an onlooker began chanting, "Dear God,
dear God, dear God …"

In the split seconds of the reception turning into a wake,
Mary Ann stood frozen to her spot. The sight of her new
but now deceased husband sprawled out on the ground with
cake and icing covering him, hadn't produced panic just
stunned numbness.

Now, though, Mary Ann was realizing what the coroner
would later confirm that Jimbo had suffered a massive
coronary. She became aware as Jimbo lay there surrounded
by his friends that he wasn't getting back up.

Being the practical trailer park hussy she was, Mary Ann began calculating the math in her mind on just how much it would cost to get out of St. Clair. So it was figures running through her mind that she was preoccupied with when she kneeled down to reach Jimbo.

The men naturally moved aside, making room for her, but then were stunned when Mary Ann quickly did a 30 second check for a pulse, then proceeded to take the car keys out of Jimbo's tuxedo, and the wallet from his back pocket.

"We all need to say a word of prayer as we wait for the ambulance," Rev. Hasbro, who'd rushed to the front when the commotion started, used his sermon voice attempting to bring calm to the chaos. Trouble was none of the guests were tuning in. All eyes, great and small, were fixated on Mary Ann.

The lady, who had been a bride for little over an hour and a widow for less than two minutes, tossed her mother the keys. "Start it up, momma!"

With a smoothness that made it seem like it'd been part of the rehearsal process, Mary Ann grabbed a nearby shopping bag one of the guests had brought their gift in, and with one fell swoop, slid the cards stuffed with checks and cash into it.

"Can she do that?" Cole asked wondering if he was the only one feeling a little queasy with what he was witnessing.

"It's her stuff. I mean, she is the bride or *was* the bride. I imagine she can do whatever she pleases," Monique answered.

Grabbing the bag with one hand, and a couple of the largest gifts on the table including the Tarkington's toaster, Mary Ann dashed for the emergency exit. She hit the metal bar on the exit like a bull coming out of the chute, bolting for the Chevrolet her mother was revving up at the curb.

Instinctively, the guests were like a group of pedestrians watching a train derail at a crossing and moved toward the windows and the exit door. They were in time to witness Mary Ann nearly tripping over her dress. The escapee to freedom paused long enough to kick off her shoes and finish the dash barefoot. Tossing the gifts into the back seat, Mary Ann with her mother as getaway driver, jolted forward with a backfire and proceeded to squeal the tires down the road leaving all the gawkers left behind with enough gossip for the next year.

It had been the last Mary Ann intended anyone in St. Clair to see of her. Unfortunately, for her, fuel filters on old Chevrolets aren't eternal. On the edge of town, mother and daughter found themselves coasting to the shoulder of the road.

Officer Sanchez was listening to dispatch give updates on the situation at the Shriner's hall and still thinking about the couple he pulled over for speeding earlier, when he noticed a woman in a wedding dress kicking the side of a beat up Chevrolet.

It took the rest of the day, some intensive questioning of the bride and her mother, a preliminary report from the Medical Examiner who had to be called in on a Saturday, and a ruling by the District Attorney from his lake house, to verify that Mary Ann actually hadn't broken any laws. Mary Ann and her mother were freed in time to catch the 10 p.m. Greyhound to Indianapolis.

As the ambulance pulled up to the Shriner's hall, and paramedics hustled in with a gurney, Monique picked the discarded shoes off the ground. Sizing them up next to her own foot, she determined they might be a good fit. She concluded it was a fair trade for the toaster.

CHAPTER 3: Sis. Gladys

"No sir, it isn't just you, the cable service is out in your whole neighborhood," Monique explained into the microphone on her headset.

"I understand that you're missing the whole second half of your game but I can assure you, crews are working to solve the problem as we speak." The answer didn't suffice the customer who let a tirade of profanity flow freely in her direction.

Only semi-cloaking her anger, Monique's voice volume raised a pitch, "Sir, there is absolutely no reason to use that kind of language with me. It's not my fault you can't see your game."

"I know this is the cable company." Monique was almost shouting now prompting a set of eyes to peer over the top of her cubicle. "But despite any misconceptions you might have, we don't control the weather. So if a bolt of lightning strikes a transformer, or say your house, there's not much we can do about that is there?"

"Sure, you can speak to my supervisor. Why not? Hold please, while I transfer you now." Monique clicked the mouse switching the call and then yanked off her headset, tossing it down on the desk in disgust.

She'd lost her temper. She'd say that was rare but lately flashes of anger, highlighted by impatience, were creeping into her persona on all levels. With Eric, she found herself cast as the grumpy mom tired of running errands, snapping at him about putting down the Wii, doing his homework or cleaning his room.

Even with Cole there'd been fights over silly things. One evening they actually fought over whether to reheat leftovers in the fridge or order a delivery from the local 'slap some cheese on the marina and call it pizza' joint, 'Top This Pizza'. In the end, Cole took Eric to McDonald's while a pouting Monique munched on the remains of a bag of celery sticks in the fridge. Even The ranch dressing she dipped the celery in didn't erase the fact she went to bed hungry that night.

Cole tried kissing to make up before turning out the lights but her lips were parched from the scorching emotional isolationism and so they remained steadfastly sealed, unable to mesh with those of whom they'd so easily said *I Do* years ago.

Monique had accepted the job at the regional cable call center simply because it meant a steady paycheck. Within a couple of months of having closed the doors on her travel business, she'd been forced to look for fresh employment.

The bills from her old business and the mortgage payment on the house demanded she'd find other employment quickly. The house wasn't upside down but Cole and she knew couples in the church whom that had happened too already. In this economy, nothing was certain.

Being thrust, unemployed, into what seemed like a jobless economy was a frightening proposition. Fortunately, Sis. Gladys, a member of the Missions Board at the church arranged for an interview with the cable company where she worked. The interview, thanks in large part to Sis. Gladys' recommendation landed Monique her job at the call center.

While low paying, it assisted in keeping the family afloat. Still, the constant negativity associated with her work was wearing her spirit down. There was a looming sense she was stuck in a rut, unable to claw her way back out to daylight. When she'd married Cole, the expectations for herself had been starkly higher.

With a fresh coffee that tasted like it'd been brewed the night before Monique returned to her terminal. On her BlackBerry, she updated her Facebook status, *"How much longer can I keep this up?"* It sounded desperate but it beat standing up and screaming like a lunatic. After another sip, she fielded the next call.

. . . . . .

Cole was holding Monique firmly. In his grasp, she felt reassured that he'd never let go. They had made an impromptu dance floor at the Café Le Saint Flaceau when Elton John's *Something About The Way You Look Tonight* began playing. Oddly, she wasn't embarrassed by his offer to dance and didn't hesitate in accepting the invitation when he said, "Why not?"

Why not indeed! Monique thought clasping Cole's hand and stepping out onto the floor. She hadn't been the same since they met and she knew from the knot in her stomach her life had taken a sharp left turn on a road where there were no u-turns.

Other tables observed their amateurish moves as the song played. One younger couple was chuckling though the source of the laughter was as much about the song as Cole and Monique's dancing skills.

A stiffer couple, who'd exchanged only a handful of words to each other over their elegant meal, eyed Cole and Monique with a judgmental gaze before silently resuming picking away at their roasted pork which had been the special of the house.

Still, a third couple rose from their seats half-way through the second chorus and with a little shrug joined Cole and Monique. The proprietors, looking on seemed genuinely thrilled to have happiness waltzing the isles of their establishment. Happiness tended to attract customers and sure enough before the song ended, two couples who stopped to peer inside, liked what they saw and decided to take a table.

In Cole's arms, Monique experienced a comfort zone. Wherever, they were twirling to, she didn't mind. When he whispered in her ear that he loved her and wanted her to come to America, she smiled, kissed him ever so slightly on the cheek and rested her chin on his collar bone.

.   .   .   .

"As I was saying ..." Sis. Gladys started.

"Would you like another coke?" Monique interjected not so much out of politeness as wanting an excuse to duck into the kitchen because she sensed what was coming next.

"No, dear, one is enough," Sis. Gladys answered as though denying herself the joys of an extra coke, even a diet one, protected a figure that when placed on the scales of life had already been let go too long to bring the needle back down to marginal digits. Her hands slid downward straightening out her floral patterned dress where the yellow daisies seemed inordinately large.

"I'll pass too," Sis. Gladys' husband, Douglas Hackworth told Monique before there was a chance to ask.

Monique noticed that Douglas kept rubbing his gray mustache and fidgeting with his blue business suit while glancing down at his shiny gold Omega watch as though anxious for the point to be made. He just wanted to return home, pop two sleeping pills, and doze off for the night.

"How about you, Bill?" Monique's eyes were pleading for the minister to bail her out.

Rev. Hasbro held up his still half-full glass and Monique resigned herself to staying put.

"As co-chairs of the Missions board, well that sounds so formal doesn't it?" Cole thought modesty wasn't Sis. Gladys' best act.

"Maybe, just a tad," Rev. Hasbro stated.

"We're hanging in suspense, dear," Douglas said dryly.

"Well, the thing is see, we've been authorized to come here this evening, by the Missions board, to say we'd like you to make one more trip,"

Where to now? Monique wondered.

Cole cleared his throat. "Last time I met the board, I thought I made it clear that I wouldn't be making any trips for a while. I don't mind somewhere down the line."

Rev. Hasbro interjected, "No, you don't understand. Sis. Gladys isn't talking about another missions trip. Well, she is but not really. I mean, this isn't being financed by our arrangement with the Global Missions Group."

"Oh, Lord no!" Sis. Gladys exclaimed with a chuckle that made her whole body shake. Douglas bounced slightly from the vibration of the couch they were sharing and rolled his eyes.

"You've done enough. Well, I think you've done enough anyway. That whole Ukraine thing, well that wasn't your fault now was it? Besides, we have so many projects going at the moment - it's so time consuming if I say so myself," Sis. Gladys explained.

"And as the representative on the Regional Board for Global Missions, I think I can say pretty assuredly that last minute projects after that Ukraine fiasco are frowned on these days," Rev. Hasbro declared.

"Maybe, you should tell the Tarkington's what you have in mind," Douglas prodded knowing it was important to let the co-chair, his wife, have her moment no matter how long it took her to come around to the point.

"Yes, yes, you're right. Well, see, we thought we would reward you, both of you, for your sacrifice. You know of our tour to the Holy Land?"

Monique sighed, "We just can't afford it. We've already had this discussion with Rev. Hasbro, several times. Bill?"

"Hear her out," Rev. Hasbro calmly urged.

"Yes, yes. See, this is a gift. The trip won't cost you anything. That's the beauty of it," Sis. Gladys explained excitedly.

"I'm confused," Cole said.

"That makes two of us," Monique added.

Sis. Gladys started to explain, "See, Jimbo- wasn't that so sad? Right there at the reception? Tsk, tsk. tsk."

Monique glanced down at her beige shoes and then slid her feet under the coffee table hoping no one noticed.

Sis. Gladys continued, "Jimbo had all the best intentions with that girl. Wasn't that disgraceful the way she took off like that? Who would act in such a manner? And his funeral, earlier this week, I was a little embarrassed there was such a small crowd there but not half as embarrassed as those pallbearers who dropped the casket. Poor Jimbo can't catch a lucky break even in death. You know, I heard his wife …"

"Maybe we shouldn't repeat rumors and keep the subject on why we're here," Rev. Hasbro advised.

"Yes, Gladys. For pete's sake, get to the point," Douglas urged.

"I am getting the point, dear. You're right, Pastor. You're so right. People do talk. Who knows what is true or isn't. Still, Jimbo, the kind big hearted soul, held the best intentions. He bought him and his new bride two tickets for the tour. A little honeymoon present for the two of them, I guess. Personally, I found it romantic, myself," she glanced over to Rev. Hasbro who nodded his consent.

"But it seems," Sis. Gladys continued, "that fatal heart attacks aren't covered by travel insurance especially when there's no next of kin to provide the paperwork and the airline refuses to issue a refund. Do you know I was on the phone with them for an hour the other day? Most of it on hold. It takes forever to get a live human being on those calls. I'm certainly glad the cable company doesn't work that way."

Monique caught herself before popping off at that remark.

Douglas interrupted, "The bottom line is, since we're stuck with the tickets anyway, the board convened a short emergency meeting as you'd have it and made the motion that we give the tickets to you, Cole, and Monique as a way of saying thank you for all your hard labors. Consider it an early tax-deductible Christmas gift."

"We do appreciate your work and hopefully this little gift will express our gratitude," Rev. Hasbro said.

Cole politely responded, "That is awful generous but ..."

Rev. Hasbro held up his hand to interrupt. "There is a catch."

"What kind of catch?" Cole sensed a real whopper coming down the pike.

"We need to bring our Mission's program into the modern age. Something that will appeal to young participants and get the message out at the same time," Rev. Hasbro explained.

"I love this part." Sis. Gladys remarked. "You know that reality shows are all the rage these days. Well, we're going to make our own!"

"You're what?" Cole stammered.

"You can't be serious?" Monique was stunned.

"Well, who wouldn't want to be in a reality show?" Sis. Gladys declared.

"Anyone with an IQ above 10." Monique countered.

"Mo is right. Where did you come up with this, this ... "

51

Douglas held steadfast, "Cole, the board has made up its mind. A reality show will be fun to watch. We have an outlet to peddle the product if we can shoot a couple shows. It will attract young people and draw them into participation. Financing has been approved."

"The board thought that filming in the Holy Land would be a great draw. I think they are right," Rev. Hasbro told Cole.

"Then you're as crazy as they are," Cole observed.

"The board wants you to on the trip, have yourselves a good time. The tickets are free after all but while there just take some time to meet with a coupe officials and see what it will take to film there," Douglas explained.

There was a stunned pause before Sis. Gladys declared, "That's that, I guess."

Sis. Gladys downed the rest of her coke and promptly stood up catching the Tarkington's and Rev. Hasbro off-guard although Douglas almost beat her up off the couch.

Monique slipped off her shoes under the table before standing up. "What do you mean that's it?"

"Oh, we'll email you the trip details tomorrow," Sis. Gladys told her.

Douglas turned to Monique in his usual business posture and added, "Don't worry, hotels and everything are included in the package. You just have to bring yourselves, really."

Cole saw red rising up in Monique's face. "I think what Mo is saying is that it isn't quite that simple, right?"

"Right," Monique declared. "To begin with, what makes you think we want to star in some reality show?"

"You don't have to star in it if you don't want," Rev. Hasbro assured. "Just check out the details for us and if you want no further involvement when you get back, then fine. That will be that."

"It isn't just us. There's Eric, for instance," Cole quickly pointed out. "We'd have to make arrangements."

"I'm sure you can get someone to watch him," Sis. Gladys stated rather of matter-of-fact.

"It may not be that simple, Sis. Gladys." Rev. Hasbro had intervened for he too could sense Monique's fuse burning.

"Oh, don't be silly. That boy is such an angel you'll have people standing in line to watch him," Sis. Gladys rebutted.

"Maybe, you'd like to watch him? After 24 hours you might change your mind," Monique sarcastically retorted.

"Oh, I'd love too but I'm going on the trip," Sis. Gladys announced.

"I'm seeing to that," Douglas said.

Sis. Gladys beamed, "Yes, Douglas here offered to pay my way."

"A romantic getaway?" It sounded absurd even as Cole uttered the words.

"No, I have to stay. Banking never stops," Douglas replied with a sly smile.

For the first time, the expression on Monique's face caused Sis. Gladys to sense the plan might be on the verge of going awry. "What's the matter, don't you want to go?"

Monique retreated. "It isn't that. What about work? They aren't very well going to want to let me off for a couple of weeks to roam the Middle East."

Sis. Gladys gathered herself. Her expression was as though she was about to tell a child his dog just was run over by a car. "I hate to be the one breaking this too you, dear, dear Monique. And please, don't tell anyone I did, I could lose *my* job, but I'm afraid you're going to have more free time than you planned."

"What? What are you saying? Am I losing my job?" Monique wasn't the only one taken back. Both Cole and Rev. Hasbro were stunned.

Cole repeated the question, "She's losing her job?"

"I don't know if she is going to lose it but it seems they feel a little suspension is in order. Did you really post "*How much longer can I keep doing this?"* on your Facebook account?" Sis. Gladys asked.

Monique had to think a minute. "Yeah, I guess I did. So, what? Are they reading my Facebook messages, now?"

"Yes, dear, they are. They read everyone's. I thought you knew that. You should really check your privacy settings," Sis. Gladys replied.

"They can't do that. Who are they? Big Brother?" Monique stormed.

"Dear, they can do whatever they like. They're the cable company. Look, a little time off will do you good. Take the trip. When you come back, I am sure things will have blown over and you'll be all fresh." Sis. Gladys reached for the door.

Cole motioned with his eyes to Rev. Hasbro who quickly took the cue. "Well, we'll be in touch. It will be ok, Mo."

"Yes, come on Gladys." Douglas opened the door showing her the way.

As the door shut behind the guests, Monique shook her head and stalked into the kitchen where she tackled the chore of cleaning the dishes. Cole watched her from a distance. He knew it was going to be a long night.

.   .   .   .

The lights were out. In his mind, Cole tried to imagine, without looking, how many seconds had actually ticked off the alarm clock sitting on the dresser stand next to the bed.

Cole lay still, avoiding even a twitch for fear that the rustling of the sheets might give away his position like prey playing passive to avoid the predator. There was a jab from a heel next to him that brought on a little grunt.

"Sorry, honey," Monique apologized. She used her fist to fluff the pillow for reassurance which only endured for approximately 30 seconds before she was sitting up, reaching over and flipping the light on for the sixth time since the couple had retired for the night.

Cole glanced over to the clock. Yep, that is what he thought. Less than two minutes between lights going off and going back on.

"I know it's late, honey," Monique quipped.

"Oh, it's ok." Cole was fully aware that it was the only answer he could give without eliciting a lethal response.

"It's just nothing is going right." Monique needed to hear herself state the obvious.

"Don't worry about the job. Sis. Gladys said it's only a suspension." He'd reminded her of this countless times already but patience was a virtue, right?

"You know, I don't even care about the job anymore. I hate that job. I only took it because we need the money."

"True. But remember, the fact that we need the money really hasn't changed." Cole wasn't sure where her thoughts were headed now.

"It's making me grumpy. I mean, I'm snapping at everyone. People at work, Sis. Gladys although she gets on my nerves at just about any time."

"She does have that capacity. I pity, Douglas. Not sure how he takes it," Cole said.

"Poor, Eric. Do you think he's starting to resent me? I've been so dictatorial with him lately."

Cole rolled over putting his hand on her leg. "He's not going to resent you. You haven't been that harsh."

"So, I have been harsh? I knew it," Monique exclaimed.

"That's not what I'm saying," Cole insisted.

"What are you saying then?"

Cole explained, "You're just a typical mom. That's the only point I was making. You're a typical mom and these things happen to typical moms."

"Oh, great! Just what every mom wants to hear."

"No, I mean this is the way it's supposed to be. Really, trust me, it's not that bad," Cole assured her.

Monique slapped Cole's hand away. "You're just saying that to make me feel better."

"Yes, but what do you want me to say? You know I hate sleeping on the couch. It has that lump on one side."

"I've been mean to you too." She confessed with her eyes peering out from under her bangs as though for an appeal for mercy.

"True." Cole cautiously admitted. "But I know you're just going through a rough patch. Maybe you just need to find yourself again. Maybe we should take the trip. What could it hurt?"

"What could it hurt? No, what might possibly go wrong with putting our family on television?" Monique groaned.

"They said we don't have to be in the show. All we have to do is check out details for them. How hard could that be?"

Monique shot Cole a look of disbelief. "Of course we'll have to be in it. Who else are they going to get? Checking on the arrangements is just a pretense to suck you in. Look at what happens to all those people on reality shows. They become freaks! I don't want to end up like that. Besides, I thought you didn't want to go?"

"I didn't but now we have the free tickets so why not? I'm on summer vacation. It will give you a break and I think that is what you need. A couple of weeks off doing something else besides dealing with this place might be the best prescription for you. A change of scenery can't hurt. What do you say?"

"What about the show?" Monique asked.

"I'll find the information they want and then when we get back tell them we have prior commitments. In the meantime, we'll have had a free vacation."

"That sounds devious," Monique said.

"No more devious than trying to trick us into this whole thing. What do you say?" Cole replied.

"Yes? No? Maybe? Ugh. Why don't I want to make this trip? I use to love to travel." Monique remembered how the only reason she ever came home before she met Cole was to catch 48 hours of sound sleep and do laundry so she'd have something to wear that didn't smell like a Moroccan casbah.

"What is wrong with me? I should be jumping at this chance," Monique said.

"You just haven't done it in a while, that's all. Look at it this way, if we go, it will make the trip seem that much more enjoyable. It'll be like old times for you." Cole's reasoning was difficult for Monique to resist.

"I just feel so empty right now," Monique confessed.

"Then this will give you a chance to figure out a way to fill that void, away from here and all the hassles."

"What about, Eric?" Monique asked.

"He'll probably be glad to be rid of his cruel, dictatorial mother," Cole playfully answered. Another light slap from Monique made him grin.

"I hear there are beaches in Israel," Cole hinted.

"True," Monique said.

"Beaches with lots of sun."

"I could work on my tan," Monique said.

"I could help with that."

Monique smiled for the first time in hours, "I bet you would. You're awful anxious there fellow."

"We could conspire to turn the trip into a personal jaunt just for the two of us," Cole suggested.

"With all those people from the church tagging along? With Sis. Gladys looking over our shoulders and judging our every move?" Monique pointed out.

"Ignore them."

"Yeah, right." Monique smirked.

"No, I'm serious," Cole insisted. "We go on this trip. We squeeze every moment of quality time we can from it and just enjoy each other."

Monique considered the proposition for a second. "Think it will work?"

"No work. No Eric. We leave the money worries at home. We'll be just a husband and wife exploring the land of ancient prophets and modern Israel together," Cole said.

"All that history there, you're going to have a field day," Monique concluded.

"I know," Cole confessed holding back his glee.

"Just promise me that it won't be all ancient crusader castles or so-so is buried here, Dr. Time. I want some old fashioned courting and showing the girl a good time. "

"Deal," Cole promised.

Monique slid back down into the bed and laid her head onto Cole's chest.

"I just need to find myself. Something to make me feel like the Monique you married, again."

"It'll come to you." Cole ran his hand through her hair.

"I know. But thank you, anyway."

"For what?" Cole asked.

"This," Monique replied.

"It's why we have each other, right?"

"A lot of husbands would've ditched me for a wife who has her act together," Monique observed.

"And a lot of wives would've run off to the mountains to find some guru to help them discover themselves."

"I thought about it but I can't do the yoga," Monique replied.

"Want to turn off the light?" Cole asked.

"Nah, leave it on. I don't want the promise disappearing with the dark." Monique drifted off from emotional exhaustion wondering where the next guided steps in life would lead her.

CHAPTER 4: The Four Sisters

ACTS 8:

[6] And the multitudes with one accord heeded the things spoken by Philip, hearing and seeing the miracles which he did. [7] For unclean spirits, crying with a loud voice, came out of many who were possessed; and many who were paralyzed and lame were healed. [8] And there was great joy in that city.

[9] But there was a certain man called Simon, who previously practiced sorcery in the city and astonished the people of Samaria, claiming that he was someone great, [10] to whom they all gave heed, from the least to the greatest, saying, "This man is the great power of God." [11] And they heeded him because he had astonished them with his sorceries for a long time. [12] But when they believed Philip as he preached the things concerning the kingdom of God and the name of Jesus Christ, both men and women were baptized. [13] Then Simon himself also believed; and when he was baptized he continued with Philip, and was amazed, seeing the miracles and signs which were done.

It was an age when fear of the late-night knock on the door permeated the thoughts of believers gathered at the dinner table. If a Yeshua addition to the Shabbat prayer was added, many lowered their voices least a neighbor overhear and alert the priestly hierarchy which had undertaken a campaign to wipe out the Christian sect. Those responsible for carrying out the campaign weren't restricted by limitations. Since the death of Jesus, the priests had been emboldened and arrest usually led to torture, prison, and more often than any authority would admit, death.

Even in this atmosphere of persecution, the infancy of Christian faith was maturing into a worldwide movement. The Church under the leadership of apostles like Peter, James, and John, was dispatching messengers out to the towns and villages of Roman occupied Judea and Samaria. In the wake of those messengers, converts sprung up.

The messenger who'd made a mark for himself early on, was the deacon Philip soon to be known in church circles and beyond as Philip The Evangelist. He'd been a member of the first batch of deacons appointed by the church leaders, along with the likes of contemporaries like St. Stephen, who'd felt that the charity work they were engaged in, such as feeding the people, was an essential work of God's to keep going. The economy under Roman rule, combined with constant rebellions and civil unrest, had ruptured into a schism of inequality between the classes leading to frequent hunger and the general destruction of quality of life among the masses. Wishing to avoid any appearance of impropriety, church leaders determined that they shouldn't be directly overseeing social projects. Thus, deacons were appointed to this task.

It wasn't long before the Sanhedrin, the Jewish ruling rabbinical council of priests, saw the importance these deacons played in the functionality of the church. This group of men served as a lynchpin for they were, in many senses, the most direct link with the people. Break that link, and the council calculated they might be able to stop the growth of Christianity in its tracks.

This became clear with the stoning death of the deacon Stephen at what would later be known as the Lion's Gate. A crowd, incited in part by Sanhedrin member Saul – later to gain fame as the Apostle Paul – had set upon Stephen and violently smashed his body until it was almost unrecognizable.

The Church in Jerusalem spiraled into a state of mourning at this tragedy. However, Philip wasn't deterred. He continued carrying out his deacon duties until one day he set foot for the ancient northern capital of Samaria.

Navigating the mountain roads of Samaria weren't the only challenges to Philip in preaching to the region. As he wound his way up the narrow paths overlooking the central part of the country, and where a single misstep sent a weary traveler careening to his death, he couldn't help pondering on the inexplicable belief that the region had always been in the grasp of ungodly forces.

It was here that the house of Omri, with its mysterious origins, rooted its capitol in ancient times. It was in Samaria, King Ahab murdered a landlord because he dared to refuse to sell his property and where Ahab's Phoenician-born queen, Jezebel, allowed the worship of Baal to flourish with her royal blessing.

But then, like now, the times brought forth messengers of deliverance. First, Elijah defeated and slayed the priests of Baal while his equally powerful student, Elisha, having blessed the warrior Jehu, watched as prophecy was fulfilled. Jehu seized the moment of liberation the region by slaughtering every son of Ahab's thus ending the House of Omri forever. Jezebel, destined by history to be synonymous with debauchery, found herself tossed from the palace walls where dogs devoured her body. Only the legend of her treachery lingers.

It was in the highlands of Samaria the Jewish faith found an earlier separation. A second temple had been constructed and a rival priesthood to the one in Jerusalem took root. The Samaritans hadn't marched to Jerusalem's beat since the Kingdom of Israel split into two.

Even now, Philip learned he was entering a region under the thumb of a renowned sorcerer. One who had manufactured his reputation through trickery and deceit. His name was Simon and he wasn't giving up his public pedestal without a struggle. The people held a fearful measure of respect for him and he intended to keep his stature.

Still, for the moment, Philip set aside the worries about Simon. For Philip, this was as much a journey wrapped an introspective urge as completion of a calling. Philip was well aware that many believers back in Jerusalem were partaking in the dusty march up the mountain with him in spirit.

Philip walked a few yards from the towering Roman theatre dominating the city's landscape. It was built to help bring back some of Samaria's illustrious glory. The structure graced the landscape with its circular design and acoustic brilliance, allowing sounds to reverberate off the mountains. Philip turned his back on the majestic monument and approached with timidity an unremarkable place marking John the Baptist's final resting spot.

It was at the Palace in Samaria that John The Baptist, the forerunner of the faith, had been beheaded at the whim of a dancer who'd held a lustful, fool-hearty king, to his careless promise. The ground of Samaria had once again been drenched with the blood of the innocent.

For Philip, and many of the apostles, the teachings of John the Baptist had led them down the path to following Jesus. The connection was undeniably strong and the wound of the heart brought on by John's death still was fresh for many believers. Their devotion couldn't be denied even by the counting of days. Paying a silent homage was the least Philip could do and he couldn't help, while dwelling in that inner space of solace, wondering in the back of his mind if a similar fate awaited him.

His efforts in Samaria proved to be a success. Despite Simon's warnings, the Samaritans flocked to hear Philip speak. In droves, they converted to the faith and Philip, the deacon who'd been striving in the shadow of others

*back in Jerusalem, was tagged with the moniker, 'The
Evangelist'.*

*Simon watched from a distance as his grip on the
people's superstitious minds was loosened. Simon also
witnessed in wonder a power built on truth as opposed to
the trickery he'd learned to master. In the end, he too
became a convert.*

.   .   .   .

ACTS 8:

**[26] Now an angel of the Lord spoke to Philip, saying,
"Arise and go toward the south along the road which
goes down from Jerusalem to Gaza." This is desert. [27]
So he arose and went. And behold, a man of Ethiopia, a
eunuch of great authority under Candace the queen of
the Ethiopians, who had charge of all her treasury, and
had come to Jerusalem to worship, [28] was returning.
And sitting in his chariot, he was reading Isaiah the
prophet. [29] Then the Spirit said to Philip, "Go near and
overtake this chariot."**

*The problem with success, Philip soon discovered, was
that just when you think you can sit back and rest on your*

laurels, events pull you in like a whirlwind forcing you to step up to a level higher than where you had been before.

Philip was at home in Jerusalem when a voice told him to take the road to Gaza. A logical man would've found reason not to make the journey for the road led through a desolate stretch of desert dotted only by small villages. On the surface, there was no reason to go.

One thing Philip had learned in working with spiritual matters was to let go of 'reason.' If the voice said 'go', it was time to go. So he took to the road not necessarily knowing what he was looking for or what awaited him.

With the scorching earth beneath his feet, and a solar torch in the sky above his head, Philip walked his way toward destiny which he found in the form of an Ethiopian Eunuch riding his chariot home from Jerusalem.

The Eunuch was no ordinary Ethiopian. The muscular warrior wore the trappings of royal office for he was in charge of the Queen's treasury. The Ethiopians had been bonded to Israel and Judaism since the torrid affair between Solomon and the Queen of Sheba had threatened to destroy both kingdoms.

As it so happened, the Eunuch was lost in translation – literally. He was trying to understand Jewish scriptures and Philip's presence provided a translator. Before it was over, Philip found himself baptizing the Ethiopian. This was, in real historical terms, the first gentile convert to Christianity recorded. It was an event that allowed Ethiopians to lay claim to the title of the 'first Christians' a source of pride in their cultural heritage.

On the surface, this episode rated as remarkable if it had ended with the baptism and Philip had returned to Jerusalem with the happy news of what had transpired. However, the most amazing feat was still to come.

Immediately upon finishing with the Ethiopian, Philip was whisked away by the Spirit and found himself in Azotus. From there he preached his way up the coast until he came to Caesarea Maritme where he settled down. After this, nothing surprised Philip anymore.

. . . .

Acts 21:

[8] On the next *day* we who were Paul's companions[a] departed and came to Caesarea, and entered the house of Philip the evangelist, who was *one* of the seven, and stayed with him. [9] Now this man had four virgin daughters who prophesied.

"What are you doing here, ma'am?" the strangely clad man asked Monique.

"I don't know," she answered, glancing about her surroundings which were as alien to her as an Eskimo finding himself in the Sahara.

"Do you have a name?" the man politely inquired.

"Yes." She stared at the buildings which from her trips to Italy and North Africa she recognized as being sorta Roman but still, sorta not.

"Would you mind sharing your name?" The man felt a little perplexed on why the stranger seemed so confused.

"Oh, yes. Sorry. Monique."

"Monique ... Monique ..." The man muttered to himself.

Monique attempted to gain control of her thoughts which seemed to slip away from her everytime she tried to concentrate. This was a dream. What would cause a dream like this? What was on TV when she and Cole fell asleep? Conan O'Brien wouldn't cause a dream like this would he? Nah, that would be something Irish or having to do with Manatee's.

Could it be something she ate? They say food influences dreams. Did she eat spaghetti? Pizza? Even a little hummus? Wait, they'd had fried chicken. Somehow, fried chicken didn't speak of ancient Rome to her.

72

"I don't think I have ever heard that name before but it has a nice sound to it. I like it," the man declared with a friendly smile that disarmed Monique instantly.

"Are you looking for something in particular?" the man inquired.

"I don't know," she admitted.

"I see," he replied.

"No, I don't think you do. I think I am dreaming is the thing. You're just a figment of my imagination," she informed him with a smile. "No offense."

"In that case, why don't you come to my home? I'd like you to meet my daughters."

She hesitated, "I don't know."

"If I'm only a figment of your imagination, what do you have to lose? A good dream should always be entertaining, yes? Besides, I sincerely believe my daughters will enjoy meeting you and you them," the man surmised.

"How many daughters do you have?"

"Four. You can meet them. Stay awhile if you wish," the man offered.

"But I'm dreaming," Monique reminded him.

"Then stay until you awake," the man suggested.

"But I don't know you," Monique hesitated.

"If it is a dream, what does it matter? But in any case, I'm Philip."

Finding truth in what he was saying and sensing she needed to see where this led her; Monique followed Philip through the busy thoroughfares of Caesarea Maritime. She was amazed by the busy crowd of people and the number of Roman clad soldiers residing in the city.

It was a reality of the times that the number of soldiers was proportionally high in Caesarea than most the rest of the country for the city had quickly become the capital of the region. The two main garrisons in the country were stationed here and in Jerusalem.

Caesarea Maritime was officially Herod's gift to the Emperor while unofficially built to be a monument to himself. Special stone had been imported to create a port in Caesarea where Mother Nature had provided it with none. Under Herod's orders, workers gave birth to the busiest port in the region.

Out of the sand dunes that shifted with the winds coming off the Mediterranean, Herod built magnificent warehouses and palaces. Before long, the Romans considered it so much a home away from home that Pontius Pilate kept his palace here.

Pilate was reputed to be short-tempered. It was well-known he had a special disgust toward Galileans brought before him. No one was sure why, but he couldn't contain his wrath toward them. However, here in Caesarea, the scene was more peaceful than the rest of the territory under his control and so it was a tentative safe haven.

That is because while Christians were endlessly pursued in Jerusalem, Caesarea was more a Roman town than a Jewish one and as such the Romans didn't bother the Christians unless there was trouble afoot. Rome's policy was one of inclusiveness although policy didn't always translate into practice.

All this meant that among the Roman arches, the aqueduct that ran water for miles for the people and crops, and the amphitheatre that had the Purple Sea as a backdrop on the horizon, a community of Christians had arisen in tentative safety.

If the port of Caesarea was a strategic location for Herod and his Roman masters, it was also a prime locale for believers. Since it was the main port, believers from around the Empire often landed here first and it was a normal occurrence for Philip to be putting up a stranger for the night. It also meant that the believers in Caesarea knew the latest news before their counterparts in Jerusalem. In many respects, Philip's abode was the worldwide hub of Christian activity.

"These are my four daughters," Philip said introducing Monique. Whenever, Philip worried about the future of the faith, all he had to do was look around his house. His daughters were that future.

If Philip had earned a bit of notoriety, then his daughters were not far behind in claiming their own reputations. They were known as women who possessed the gift of prophecy and as travelers came through, it wasn't unusual for the sisters to reveal to passing believers important information to assist them on their journey.

Prophecy is a two edged sword for the sister's weren't immune to a glimpse of their own future. They would strive on with their work even though two of them would die virgins having sacrificed the personal for the spiritual, one would raise a family elsewhere only to witness the martyrdom of those closest to her, and the fourth would disappear into historical obscurity covered forever by the sands of time.

Monique sensed she was at ease with them but there was something, she couldn't put her finger on it, that was different. Maybe she couldn't focus long enough in this fried chicken induced-state to pick up what she was missing about them. Now that she thought about it, maybe it was the chocolate chip ice cream, Eric's wish, for dessert that was bringing this sideshow into existence. Note to self; limit yourself to one scoop next time.

At Philip's behest, Monique shared olives and grapes with his family. She thought the grapes were the juiciest she'd ever tasted. It put the local farmers market to shame. How could she know all this in a dream?

Monique noticed strangers entering the space. Their faces were undefined. Their features more shadows than shapes of familiarity. Their dress more like Philip's although the dust and wear on the clothes spoke of long journeys.

Yet, the strangers tended to flock to the four sisters. Often a sister would pull a stranger aside, just beyond the horizon of Monique's imagination, and in the dark haze Monique detected inaudible whispers.

"Don't fret," Philip assured her. "They've traveled far for a comforting word".

"Travel far?" Monique replied.

"Yes. Sometimes they come from places like Alexandria, or Ephesus. We had a visitor from Messina just last month," Philip told her.

"I was in Alexandria once with a tour," Monique said unaware of why she volunteered the information. It was as though her thoughts had a voice of their own.

Philip looked a little confused by her statement but continued the conversation out of politeness.

"Are you a believer?" Philip asked.

"A believer?"

"In Jesus. Are you a believer?"

"Oh, yes, we're Christians. We attend the local church faithfully." Monique again was unsure why she was opening up to a total stranger like this. But did it matter? It was only too much ice cream speaking, right?

"Are you on the way, to Jerusalem?" Philip asked.

"Yes, we're going on a tour. How did you know?" Monique wondered.

"Do you know where you're going there? Or maybe I should ask instead if you know what you'll find there?"

"Find?" But Monique's voice trailed off. She felt a spinning sensation. Philip seemed to be pulled away as though sucked through an invisible tunnel.

In a split second, the kind of instant timing that often rules the dream world, Monique found herself surrounded by the four sisters whose eyes now seemed replaced by sharp lights that burned into her consciousness.

"You don't know what you'll find because you don't know what you're looking for, do you?" Sister One said.

Spun around again, Monique found herself facing Sister Two, "A light has shone through a door that has been opened."

"Yes, opened. I see self-awareness. An admittance that is hard to phantom for you," Sister Three muttered.

Sister Four cocked her head back and Monique felt her own head throbbing as if a migraine had descended upon her. "The soul is a deep ocean. Unchartered for most people but you, you're looking to navigate it."

Monique found herself spinning again. "Seek and you shall find," Sister One told her.

"Yes, look and you will discover," Sister Two agreed.

"Don't be afraid to step forward," Sister Three advised.

"But whatever you do, don't look back. Forward ... " Sister Four warned.

Monique sensed the room rotating round her, and the room was blurring as were the faces of the four sisters. It was as though a whirlwind was building to sweep Monique away.

"Remember, faith ..." Sister One raised her voice.

"Hope ..." Sister Two chimed in as though affirming the others.

"Love ..." Sister Three said as the crescendo built.

"And for you, most importantly, charity," Sister Four said as Monique felt herself being pulled away.

The last thing Monique heard was a cry of unison, "We'll be with you."

.   .   .   .

There was an audible gasp, as Monique sat straight up in bed. She grasped the sheets, holding on until she regained her bearings.

"What's wrong honey?" Cole asked.

Hearing her heavy breathing and not getting an immediate reply, Cole scooted himself up and switched on the light. He looked at an obviously shaken Monique.

"Are you ok?" He touched her forehead then took her clammy hand which he had to practically pry from the sheet.

"What happened? Did you have a nightmare?" he asked.

"No nightmare, just a strange dream. Nightmares are your territory, right?" she replied.

"Right," he agreed without being persuaded.

"You didn't dream of snakes, did you?" he asked.

"No! I think the ice cream was bad," Monique concluded.

"The ice cream?"

"I shouldn't have so much before bed. It upset my stomach." She slid out of bed and headed into the bathroom.

She pulled two aspirin out of the medicine cabinet which she quickly swallowed then splashed water on her face. She looked in the mirror and stared hard. She recognized the image but not was happening to her or her life.

When she re-entered the bedroom, Cole asked, "Are you ok?"

"I think we definitely have to take this trip," she declared shifting her balance from leg to leg while standing near Cole with her arms folded.

"You're sure?"

"A 100 percent." She tried hard to sound convincing. She hoped her instincts were correct as she slid back under the sheets.

"A 100 percent? Well then, who am I to argue?" Cole put his arm around his wife as she crawled back into bed.

.   .   .   .

The travel arrangements were made the next day. Cole, wishing to avoid a long entangling conversation with Sis.

Gladys, called Rev. Hasbro and informed him that the Tarkington's had changed their minds and decided to accept the generosity of the church by accepting Jimbo's vacated tickets for the Holy Land Tour. Cole assured his friend that he'd gather what info he could for the reality show.

Monique had forgotten how hard it was to pack for a trip especially when you weren't totally sure what would be needed. What if it rained? But it was the desert, right? What were the odds of it raining?

Did she suppose her and Cole might slip away for a candle light dinner somewhere? Should she take something elegant to slip on just in case? What was considered elegant in the Middle East these days?

She knew she'd be escaping to the beach at some point so the swimsuit had a special place reserved in the suitcase. She didn't try it on first. If she looked fat in it, she didn't want to know. No one knew her there anyway. She was looking forward to lying in the sand and listening to the waves lap up on the shore around her. The Middle East definitely would be a change of scenery from the Midwest.

Then there was Eric who actually didn't seem that disappointed to learn his parents would be gone for a couple of weeks. Monique suspected he anticipated later

82

bedtimes, more sweets, and a slacking off of homework with whoever was watching him.

Turns out the person stepping in to accept the long-term baby-sitting assignment was Mulu. She couldn't make the trip because of her Ethiopian passport, getting a visa would be an Olympian accomplishment, so she was happy to step in and watch Eric who had grown to like her over the months that she'd been coming to church.

For Mulu, it meant a couple weeks outside the college dorm and the comfort of a nice house. More importantly, Monique knew Mulu was responsible. If something happened, God forbid, she was sure Mulu would know how to handle it.

Mulu's presence though probably meant Randy spending time around the house and with Eric. Monique hoped Randy didn't give Eric any more music. She'd overheard Eric singing *You Really Got Me* one night in the shower. She'd laugh but at the same time it was too early a stage for her to have to start worrying about him entering the rock-n-roll phase of his life. Was he going to be a drummer or a guitar player? Please, Lord, let him fall in love with the cello.

What Monique and Cole didn't know how to handle was the airline which true to form threw a monkey wrench into their plans to make this trip about togetherness.

"I just don't understand people, sometimes." Sis. Gladys let out a rather loud sigh as she thrust Cole's and Monique's tickets into their hands.

"I tried to reason with them but they keep saying there is nothing they can do. Changing your seating assignments apparently will put someone else in the same position. I'm sorry, but the two of you just won't be able to sit together on this flight," Sis. Gladys explained.

"But we're, together," Monique stated.

"I told them you were husband and wife. Apparently, the reservation system doesn't care."

"But these are Jimbo's and what's her name's old reservations, right? I mean they would've been flying together, right?" Cole pointed out.

"Obviously, fate knew all along those two were never flying together anywhere. Kind of telling, don't you think?" Sis. Gladys observed.

"It's just one flight. You'll be together when you land. That's the important thing," Rev. Hasbro said attempting to smooth over any anxiety.

"You're right," Monique agreed.

The couple who'd set out to take a journey to reignite their togetherness found themselves being scanned into seats rows apart from each other. Cole found himself buckled in beside a mother with a 2-year-old. Monique was next to a couple of Haredim with their dark clothes and wide-brimmed hats looking like they'd been bought at an 18th century clothing store in Hamburg. She found herself starring in amusement at the curly sideburn locks hanging down the side of their faces. The Haredim ignored everyone and wasted no time. They began mouthing prayers the moment they sat down. Monique turned on her iPod to shuffle away the plane's distractions.

CHAPTER 5: Out Of The Shell

In Yafo, Israel, tucked away in the old neighborhood commonly referred to as the American Colony a well kept building housed a religious congregation. The congregation operated a public guest house catering mostly to pilgrims passing through on their way to Jerusalem, in the same manner that residents of Yafo had been housing pilgrims and Zionists for a couple of thousand years. A century ago visitors debarked from a ship in the city's port. Now days, they arrived via taxi from Ben Gurion International Airport.

The congregation's building stood out in the neighborhood not so much in design (in fact it was near impossible from the outside to determine anything religious was occurring inside) as by the sheer fact the facility was kept in decent condition. In contrast, across the street from it lay the gutted out shell of what had once been an elaborate piece of property.

Other buildings in the neighborhood were in the process of receiving facelifts. Local land owners were racing to take advantage of what had been slated as the next big area to experience a jump in property values. Many owners aspired to flipping the properties before any future real estate bubble zapped them of their cash rich dreams.

Yafo, which to countless Westerners was better known by its biblical names of Jaffa and Joppa, had been incorporated into the city of Tel Aviv years ago with the stroke a politician's pen. Despite that, the city still maintained its own identity distancing itself from the more European flavor of Tel Aviv.

People didn't say, "I'm from Tel Aviv-Yafo." They declared they were either from Tel Aviv or they were from Yafo. The two may have been joined at the hips by the ruling establishment but Yafo possessed its own exclusive atmosphere. The buildings spoke of the 1930s, or in some cases earlier, reminding the casual onlooker of a time when Istanbul was the seat of power instead of Jerusalem.

The congregation of Beit Immanuel was the largest Messianic Jewish group within the city of Tel Aviv- Yafo. It's one-hundred plus members gathered every Friday evening like any other Jewish group in Israel honoring Shabbat.

The difference was, as members of the congregation would say that their rabbi of choice was a guy from Nazareth whom they believed to be resurrected and not a dead rabbi from Eastern Europe. More specifically, they weren't associated with any personage tied to the corrupt Rabbinate, a dinosaur of an institution with which kept its claws around the neck of the country to the point that even civil weddings were illegal and a citizen's Jewishness was questioned on a daily basis. Things were so bad; remnants of families which had been nearly extinguished in the Holocaust were often told they didn't qualify as being Jewish.

Members of Beit Immanuel knew all too well about having their Jewishness questioned. All the patrons with only a handful of exceptions were from families that immigrated to Israel in the last quarter-of-a-century. A majority were of Russian or Nordic descent.

The fact they worshiped Jesus, or Yeshuva as he was known in Hebrew, was bad enough but the fact their bloodlines flowed into the Promised Land from places like Moscow, Stockholm, and Helsinki compounded the disgrace in the eyes of an Orthodoxy who were so racially prejudiced that East European Haredim rioted in the streets when their students were forced to study with Orthodox Jews who descended from places like Spain, Yemen or Morocco. The only thing that all the Orthodox religious groups agreed upon regardless of their ancestry was that anyone with dark skin from south of the Sahara had no place at all in their ranks.

The Orthodox weren't passive in their beliefs either.
Messianic Jews took security precautions when holding
services. The worshipers at Beit Immanuel felt relatively
safe but groups in places like Beer Sheeva had their
services disrupted by rampaging Orthodox mobs. In one of
the most extreme instances, the child of a preacher had
opened what he thought was a Purim gift basket only to
have a bomb explode in his hands.

Under such circumstances, if you were attending Beit
Immanuel it was pretty much assumed you were a believer.
Consequently, the atmosphere was relaxed, almost to the
point of being too informal but it was one of the aspects
Yossi enjoyed about it; a total lack of pretensions.

Yossi had been steered to the congregation by someone at
the hospital. He'd had to look up their website on the
internet for directions but eventually found his way there.

The opening of the service itself was steeped in Jewish
ceremony with the leader of the congregation inviting a
couple of the women to the front for the traditional lighting
of the candles and the reciting of the accompanying Jewish
prayer that had congregational participation.

Shortly, after the ritual's was conclusion, the service
morphed into a different creature. It was more reminiscent
of an American style service back in Los Angeles where

Yossi had lived before setting on this worldwide trek which didn't seem to have an end.

A band began jamming on the platform and leading congregational songs. As in Yossi's case, if you didn't know the words, the lyrics were plastered in English, Russian, and Hebrew on a big projector screen hanging behind the band.

The congregation, including Adi and Elain who were seated next to Yossi, sang along. Adi's baritone voice was well off key and Yossi noticed he kept shifting his glasses as though that would somehow make his pitch more accurate.

Elain on the other hand, had a voice angels envied. Her short cropped blonde hair stopped just above the butterfly tattoo stenciled at the base of her neck.

Elain's excitement for the singing was encouraged by the lead singer on the platform who kept the crowd excited. She was a young lady in her twenties whose red hair was matched by the red border on her black dress and red toe nail polish on feet that kept slipping in and out of a pair of red sandals in time with the backbeat.

Yossi enjoyed the first hour of service where the music was center stage. He found it relaxing and a respite from his personal travails.

There was preaching but to a Westerner it was tame to what one might see back home. There was no John Cotton hellfire and brimstone messages or slick salesmanship. It was a typical heartfelt Israeli reasoned presentation.

The twin billing to Yossi's escapist Friday night mode was that after service ended, Adi and Elain almost always invited Yossi over for dinner at their flat. The two computer software engineers lived modestly in the city and had rather quickly taken a liking to Yossi.

"I don't get it," Elain started.

"Get what?" Yossi asked.

"Well, you should be out having fun. You should have a girlfriend. I mean it isn't like you're that old and your looks are ok."

"Gee, thanks," Yossi said.

"Well, it's not good to be alone you know. I mean, are you having trouble meeting girls? Maybe I could introduce you to a couple," Elain suggested.

"Elain!" Adi tried intervening to save his friend.

"I'm just trying to help! Is all you do is work at the hospital? Don't you ever have any fun?" Elain queried.

"Good question." Yossi took a small piece of fish from a plate Adi passed him.

"Is there a good answer?" Elain pressed.

"Probably not," Yossi confessed.

"He's a doctor. He's busy. People are always needing medical attention," Adi interjected.

"It is steady employment," Yossi joked.

"I'm just saying … "

"We know what you're saying. We get it," Adi countered.

"It's ok. Elain is probably right. I probably need to get out and socialize more," Yossi admitted.

"Just go see something. I mean Israel is full of sites," Elain said.

"True. True. I've been meaning to check out the Ben Gurion house," Yossi stated.

Elain laughed. "You'll need something livelier than that if you want to impress a lady."

Yossi smiled, "Yeah that wouldn't exactly be a jumping joint would it?"

"You never know. Ben Gurion was pretty crazy," Adi noted.

"I read where, despite his efforts pivotal role in building a Jewish state, he secretly ate pork for breakfast every morning," Yossi told them.

Adi shook his head in disbelief. "Ben Gurion?"

"Yeah, Ben Gurion."

"I don't believe it."

"He was a politician. What do you expect?" Elain asked.

"Listen, going back to you being a doctor and all …" Adi started.

Yossi became more attentive. Over the years, he'd learned that whenever an acquaintance approached him with a lead-in like that, something personal was coming down the pike. Often the personal was digging for free medical advice but Yossi knew Adi. This was going to be more than "I have this ache, can you prescribe something?"

Elain cut Adi off, "Not now."

"What? We're here. It's as good as time as any. He knows us. He eats here practically every Friday," Adi shot back.

Yossi brushed aside Elain's worries, "What's on your mind, Adi?"

"We have this problem," Adi started without being quite sure how to continue.

"We?" Yossi asked.

Elain, being Elain, blurted out, "We'd like to have a child."

The topic caught Yossi off-guard. However, being a doctor, he'd learned to field all kinds of requests at strange times.

"And your doctor says you can't?" Yossi asked.

"Not naturally," Adi replied.

Elain turned aside as though the very fact this had to be discussed was an embarrassment.

"I see. Well, tell you what, I will do. Let me gather up some information for you to look at. I am sure we have something around the hospital in Hebrew. Once I get that together, you can look it over and then we'll make an appointment for you to come by the office and we'll have a little chat to see if we can chart some sort of action for you to take. Does that sound ok?"

Adi smiled. "That sounds fine."

"Thanks, Yossi." Elain said but Yossi could tell something else was bothering her.

"What is it?" Yossi asked.

"Well, I don't want anyone to find out about this," she explained.

"Her parents wouldn't take it too well," Adi added.

"I see. Well, don't fret. This is strictly a doctor-patient relationship. Now, did you make any dessert?"

Elain smiled and got up from the table to take the pudding she had made out of the fridge.

CHAPTER 6: The Pool

The open air café a few meters inside Jaffa Gate was typical of what may be found in Jerusalem's Old City. The Arab owners hustled dishes, catering to the cavalcade of tourists marching past every day. Simple in their presentation, the local dishes played on the palates of the curious traveler.

Yossi, his shirt soaked with the afternoon's sweat, was sipping on a Coke Zero and witnessing the world whistle by through the lens of his sunglasses.

The Jaffa Gate was one of seven main gates to the Old City of Jerusalem. Only the Damascus Gate situated on the opposite side of the Old City rivaled it for foot traffic. For centuries, merchants had entered the presence of Jerusalem through the Jaffa Gate's towering stone structure. Between 1948 and 1967, it'd overlooked the boundary between the new State of Israel and the Hashemite Kingdom of Jordan. In the Six Day War, Israel reunified the city when it fought its way into and seized the Old City.

In the 1800s, kiosks constructed outside the gate hosted peddlers hoping to convince buyers to spend their money before they ever entered the gate. Now, in the 21st century, the kiosks had been replaced by a galleria mall which

Jewish city officials intended to shift business away from the Arab quarters but for Yossi the galleria held no appeal. In the end all the window dressing couldn't change the fact it was still a mall. He didn't like malls in the States and he despised them even more when they were built next to a treasure trove of history.

The complex of buildings just inside the Jaffa Gate that now included a tourist office and a rundown hostel/hotel, had in a distant era been the nerve center for foreign dignitaries. A hotel complex that'd been located there was where visiting foreign government officials and V.I.P.'s spent their nights. Many of the most important 19th and 20th century decisions that'd determining the course of Jerusalem's history had been formulated inside its long-ago diminished grandeur.

Yossi's mind wandered from the historical to the present as he noticed a comically dressed tourist. An overweight Englishman was parading around in white shorts that were accompanied by orange socks pulled up to his knees.

Behind the Englishman, Yossi spotted a female Islamic fundamentalist covered from head to toe. He wondered how she managed in this heat without passing out.

Yossi shut out the chatter of tourists navigating with small pocket-sized maps from the Tourist Office. Most of the tourists brushed aside local guides offering their services for a small commission.

It was his day off from Wolffsohn, where despite the assurances of David Landsberg back in Haiti, the actual amount of doctoring he'd done since his arrival had been minimal. Yossi had realized after his arrival in Israel that David and Jonas had colluded in giving him lighter, if yet meaningful, duty. It was the break that Jonas had encouraged him to take but which Jonas had known all too well Yossi wouldn't do on his own.

So, Yossi had taken Adi and Elain's advice of trying to get out and socialize. He'd been hitting all the tourist sites which got him out and about but didn't really involve much socializing. Sometimes, he repeatedly went to the same sites as though they might hold some magical piece of logic he'd overlooked on his previous visit.

It didn't matter really. Secretly, Yossi was contemplating an offer from an old acquaintance from medical school days who'd emailed him about joining his practice. It was a tempting offer. The money would be quadruple – or more – what he was taking home now. It'd be a chance to coast for a while and he'd be back in Los Angeles, well, Beverly Hills to be more precise. It'd been too long since he'd lived stateside. Now might be the right time to go back.

A few tummy tucks, tighten up the a buttocks here and there, throw in a lipo or two, not to mention a line of women waiting for breast augmentations, and compared to what he'd done in Ethiopia and Haiti, he'd be living easy street, clocking out by five and collecting big paychecks while spending off-hours down at the beach. Who knows, he might even meet someone who'd find him halfway interesting. Although, dating in Los Angeles was often less about mutual attraction and more about compatible bank accounts.

A giggle from a nearby table brought his thoughts back to the here and now. He glanced over at a nearby table where two women were sitting. From the bottles of water on the table and the falafel crumbs scattered about, Yossi guessed they'd just finished lunch.

He noticed they were staring in his direction. He cautiously scanned the cafe to see if maybe somebody behind him had caught their attention.

"No, we're looking at you," the blonde girl dressed in a pair of jeans, fashionable boots and a rose color shirt, told him. She put on her designer sunglasses denying Yossi more than a glimpse of her sea blue eyes.

The other girl, a slender soldier with her weapon slung around her neck and an orange beret tucked beneath her epaulet, had long dark hair and an olive tone to her skin indicating she was probably a Sabra. Her sandals contrasted the macho vibe given from the rest of her ensemble. Her smile signaled anticipation of Yossi's reply which he failed to give.

"My friend and I have a bet," the soldier continued.

Yossi was a little astonished. "You do?"

The soldier's friend briefly glanced away out of embarrassment before refocusing her gaze upon Yossi. "It doesn't bother you that we're sitting here gawking at you?"

"No. If that's how you want to waste your time, whom am I to complain?" Yossi responded.

The soldier cued her friend, and the pair stood up from their seats. When the blonde stood up, she revealed that even without the boots, which Yossi guessed had been picked up in Europe somewhere, she was rather tall.

The two girls walked over to his table.

The blonde asked, "Do you mind?"

She didn't wait for the answer, as she slid into a chair and gracefully took a seat. The soldier sat next to her allowing the rifle to rest in her lap. Yossi noticed loaded magazines strapped to the rifle, ready to be slapped into place at a moment's need.

Yossi pointed at the soldier, "You're in a combat unit?"

The soldier shook her head, "No, the Home Command. I mostly pass out gas masks to civilians. But I didn't have anywhere to leave my weapon today so I had to bring it along. Rules."

"Regulations are like that," Yossi commented.

"Now tell me, if our staring at you, and her lethal weapon doesn't bother you, then what secret thing does?" the blonde pressed.

Yossi detected a heavy accent in her voice. "What do you mean?"

"You were staring into oblivion just a moment ago. You seemed like a lost soul sitting here, by yourself, all blank-faced instead of being out sightseeing with the other American tourists," the blonde pointed out.

"How do you know I'm an American?" Yossi quizzed, knowing by now his own accent probably confirmed her suspicions.

The blonde reached across the table and picked up his Coke, slowly took a sip, then set it back down in front of him. Yossi smiled. He should've known.

The soldier slid out a ten shekel coin from her pocket and passed it to the blonde who quickly pocketed it.

"That was the bet? Whether or not I was American?"

"Don't change the subject on me. Answer my question," the blonde instructed.

"Well, I assure you, I'm no lost soul," Yossi informed his new found friend.

"Maybe a little unchartered then. Sometimes, we're all a little unsure what is inside us so we just wander in our own thoughts, hoping to discover what makes us tick."

"Yes, unchartered. Maybe," Yossi replied.

"Sometimes it takes a little faith to navigate your way through unchartered territory. Do you have faith to discover what you're looking for?"

"I know you're not the Dalai Lama, so who are you, anyway?" Yossi asked.

"I'm Desica. I work over at the Christian Information Center," she pointed to a nearby location. Yossi thought he remembered seeing the sign.

"This is my friend Lihi." Lihi, totally bemused by the give and take, offered a slight wave.

"I'm Yossi."

"It's nice to meet you, Yossi," Desica said.

"Likewise, I think."

Desica gave Yossi a slight smile. "Did you have plans for the day?"

"Well, I had intended to go to the Church of St. Anne," Yossi replied.

"Oh, I love that place. Some of the best ruins in the city and the church that is still standing there is interesting as well," Desica stated.

"That's true," Yossi concurred.

Desica looked over at Lihi, asking, "You have time?"

Lihi simply put up her hands indicating she did. Before Yossi was aware of it the trio had tossed their shekels down to cover the tab and were walking the Old City toward St. Anne's.

.   .   .   .

Traversing the Old City of Jerusalem's city streets is akin to being stuck in a time machine with half your body in the present and the other half trapped a millennium ago. The narrow streets and alleyways haven't altered their appearance radically since the Roman occupation 2000 years ago. In certain places, people walking the stone streets may look down and with the sudden realization they're walking upon stones laid during Roman or Byzantium times.

The trio brushed past Arab shopkeepers doing what Yossi referred to as the *tourist hustle*. The hawkers of trade attempted to entice them into shops with, "Hello. Hello. Where you from?"

The shops all resembled each other with their similar stock of Mother of Pearl jewelry boxes, painted plates depicting scenes from the Holy Land, and the olive wood figurines manufactured in Palestinian shops south of Jerusalem. Favorite items were the hookah pipes and chess sets. Why tourists would come all this way to buy a chess set, Yossi had never understood but almost every shop had them for sale.

If buyers wanted something unusual but more touristy, they could always opt for the T-shirt shops which would print almost any design from the Israeli soccer teams to the iconic Che'. The lettering could be printed in English, Hebrew or Arabic and in some cases two of the three. It was buyer's choice.

"Just take a look. You don't have to buy. Just look," was a favorite spiel spurted out. Once a tourist halted long enough to glance through the goods, the odds of a sale happening increased.

Lihi wasn't harassed with the lures from merchants. Dressed in her soldier's uniform, she was the living, breathing enemy. She wasn't feared as much as despised. The mutterings as she strutted by were just loud enough to let her know they were being uttered but low enough not to be understood. Taut compliance spoke of hard-heartedness while the occasional spit let loose on the ground behind her back spoke to an electrically charged political blanket hanging in the air where the least random spark might shock anyone and everyone.

Before entering the Church of St. Anne compound, Desica wanted to visit the Lion's Gate. Even more so when Lihi said, "What is the big deal about the Lion's Gate?"

The Lion's Gate, approximately a two-minute walk from St. Anne's, was so named for the pair of lion's carved atop each side of the Gate which weren't really lions at all but panthers. Legend held that Suleiman the Magnificent placed them there to commemorate the dream he experienced where he was told to rebuild the walls of Jerusalem or face certain death and destruction. Suleiman proceeded to embark on the most ambitious renovation of the Old City walls since Herod the Great, restoring glory to a city wracked by wars ranging from the Roman destruction in 70 A.D. to the Crusaders in the Middle Ages.

As Desica explained, the gate was originally known as the Sheep's Gate for sheep herds passed through headed to both the commercial market and the Temple Mount, located directly to the left upon entering the gate. At the Temple, sheep were designated for sacrifice.

While it was still referred to most often as the Lion's Gate by locals, in the West the gate had become more renown as St. Stephen's Gate emphasizing what Western culture valued most.

"I don't understand," Lihi said, "who was St. Stephen?"

"What do you know of Jesus and his disciples?" Desica asked.

"Only that Jesus caused trouble at the Temple," Lihi casually replied.

"That's it?" Yossi was taken back that someone, even if they were of a different religion, could hold such little background of an important historical figure like Jesus.

"That's all," Lihi replied.

"Yawzaaa ..." Yossi commented to no one in particular.

Lihi glared at him strangely. "What's that suppose to mean?"

Wanting to avoid sounding judgmental, Yossi shrugged and said, "Nothing."

Lihi wasn't believing him. "It meant something."

Yossi explained, "Really, nothing. I just assumed you knew more about Jesus is all."

Lihi rolled her eyes. "Oh, I grasp your meaning now. You expect me to know all about your religion when you haven't but a passing reference about mine."

"I know about Judaism," Yossi insisted.

"Really? In that case, what is your opinion of Maimonides?"

Yossi looked at her with a blank stare.

"That is what I thought." Lihi was pleased to have won her point.

Trying to rescue the situation, Desica returned to the original topic. "Let me explain," Desica offered. She proceeded to launch into a Reader's Digest length rundown of how after Jesus died, deacons and apostles were picked and Stephen was among the first group of Church leaders after the crucifixion. Desica was forced to pause long enough to explain the crucifixion as well since it was the first time Lihi had heard of it.

Desica then continued on, detailing how a Sanhedrin member named Saul incited a mob to attack Stephen at the gate. The mob descended upon Stephen with rocks, stoning him to death. Believers throughout the city mourned as they collected his body for burial. The priests, on the other hand, felt more emboldened than ever and stepped up persecution of the early church.

"All that went on in this spot?" Lihi asked a little dazed from the history lesson.

"Yes. Right where you're standing now," Desica emphasized.

"Want your picture taken?" Yossi offered. The girls posed in front of the gate with each other.

"I was just thinking. Things have changed very little since then," Desica observed.

"What do you mean?" Yossi asked.

"Well, the religious status quo is still afraid of change. Look at the riots by the mall parking lot back by the Jaffa Gate. I mean back then, they stoned Stephen because they considered themselves so religious that they had to put a man to death for holding a differing point of view. Now, they consider themselves so religious they attack the police on a Sabbath because someone drives a car," Desica explained.

"You aren't religious?" Yossi asked Lihi who rolled her eyes in response.

Like most secular Israelis, she despised the fact that a majority of Haredim – the Ultra-Orthodox - lived off government welfare and that religious students were exempted from military service, causing a hardship on the rest of society. In effect, she felt that in the house of Israel, the Haredim stayed home, complained and spent the money while the secular members of society did the grunt work to pay the bills.

As the trio walked back toward their original destination Desica asked Lihi, "How come we've never talked about any of this before?"

Lihi shrugged her shoulders.

"Well, I feel disappointed like I've let you down," Desica confessed.

"Why?" Lihi asked.

"I don't know. I guess because as a Christian we're expected to share our faith. It's part of who we are. I don't know why I never brought this stuff up to you so you would know."

"Maybe because usually we're too busy shopping," Lihi joked.

The two girls broke out in laughter.

"Oh, so true, so very true," Desica concurred.

The laughter was ignored by Yossi who'd caught a glimpse of someone as they passed by the entrance to the Temple Mount. It was an entry way only accessible to Muslims as everyone else was forced to enter from a ramp that started at the base of the Western Wall.

The person who'd caught Yossi's attention was a skinny man that in his well-worn but imported Italian shoes at best measured five foot five. The dark wavy hair that seemed frizzled could have been anyone's but the suit jacket with the gold shine to it was not a familiar site in the city which is why it stood out.

"Could it be?" Yossi questioned before shaking off the suggestion by reasoning that surely, the tailors made more than one of that design. Another person in Jerusalem could own a jacket like that. In fact, the laws of probability demanded that was the case.

"Are you drifting away on me again?" Desica asked.

"Huh?" Yossi responded.

"Are you always like this?" Desica wanted to know.

"I thought I saw someone," Yossi informed her as he watched the person disappear past the police checkpoint.

"Someone you know?" Desica asked.

"Only Muslims are allowed through that gate. You know Arabs?" Lihi inquired in a friendly voice underlined by her soldierly instincts.

"I'm sure it was someone else," Yossi said as they took a right into the courtyard of St. Anne's Church.

.   .   , ...

Monique greeted Cole who was waiting next to a terminal wall for her to disembark from the plane, "Hi, stranger."

Cole propositioned her, "Can, I interest you in a romp through the exquisitely grey gloomy terminal of Ben Gurion airport?"

"No, but you can have your way with me if you promise me a hot shower, a warm meal and soft bed."

"You sell out cheap."

"You have no idea, mister," Monique responded.

As the pair started the trek toward passport control, a familiar voice shouted out at them.

"They know me. Cole, tell this lady who I am!" Sis. Gladys had been stopped by a security person screening passengers.

"Do you know this person?" the lady in with the official badge asked.

"Yes, I do," Cole said.

"What is her name?" The lady asked, Cole.

"Gladys," Cole answered.

"Show her your passport," Monique urged Gladys.

"I can't find my passport!" Gladys exclaimed.

"You can't find your passport?" Monique almost shrieked.

"How can you lose your passport? We haven't been anywhere!" Cole exclaimed.

"It has to be on the plane but this lady won't let me go back," Gladys explained.

"You said her name is Gladys. Gladys what?"

"Gladys … " It was the long flight that caused Cole's memory to freeze up.

Finally, he said, "I don't know. We just call her Sis. Gladys."

"She is your sister but you don't know her last name?" The security lady was increasingly suspicious at this point and radioed something in Hebrew before anyone had the opportunity to dive into details.

"No, you see … "

The security lady cut Monique off. "I am sorry, ma'am. You can go on ahead. I will talk to these two."

Monique's finger drew a line between her and Cole. "But we're married."

"Please, ma'am, go on ahead to passport control."

"Go ahead honey. I will meet you on the other side. It'll be ok," Cole assured her.

With a long glare at Sis. Gladys bordering on murderous intent, Monique headed to passport control, passing along the way a security supervisor speed walking to reach Sis.

Gladys who had by now raised security alarms throughout the system.

.   .   .   .

The man in the gold jacket entered the plateau known as the Temple Mount. He walked past a group of women who had found comfortable shade under a group of trees that were working as a study group from one of the Islamic schools.

A Muslim tour group from Indonesia were stopping long enough for the tour guide to give the Islamic take on the different gateways providing access to the large acreage that consisted of the compound.

The man glanced over at the Eastern Gate. He gazed with staunch disapproval at the Christian tourists lining up to have their photo taken in front of the structure. In his opinion, they possessed no right to be on sacred ground such as the Temple Mount the same way the Jewish patrol had no right to stop him at the checkpoint.

Walking up steps through the ancient remnants of an archway, the man moved leisurely in the direction of the Dome of the Rock. The Dome, shining across the city with its gold overlay, served as a guiding beacon to the Temple

Mount. The late King Hussein of Jordan, a direct descendent from the Prophet Mohammed, had sold a mansion in London to pay for that shine. The millions he'd spent had transformed the structure into the iconic image of Jerusalem.

At the entrance to the Dome, the man smiled with pleasure as an Englishman sporting bright orange socks was turned away by two men guarding the entrance. This was an Islamic structure they informed him. Non-Muslims were barred from entering. The Englishman would have to settle for pictures from the outside or try to sneak a peek through a side entrance. No infidels allowed was the message delivered with the smile of indifference.

If the Englishman had gained access inside and was able to read Arabic then he might have been offended by the messages adorning the interior. Each wall was adorned by a message of instruction not particularly kind to Jews and especially harsh on Christians.

On the south wall was the announcement that Allah had no partners. This was meant to deter anyone who might've suggested a theological trinity applied to Allah.

Located on the southeast wall was a warning to Jews and Christians not to adhere to their own religions and that there would be dire consequences for saying anything false

113

about Allah. It pointedly declared that Jesus was only a messenger and Allah was to above the world to have provided a son.

This message was echoed on the North wall where after several blessings on Jesus the Arabic words translated that it wasn't for Allah to take any offspring. The divinity of Jesus didn't exist in the realm of Islam.

Etched on a West wall was a message that Islam was the sight of Allah or in other words, his religion of choice. And in the Northwest corner the concept of offspring was nixed yet again while reminding readers that Mohammed was the messenger of Allah.

This grudging effort to discredit all other religions, especially the ones most rivaling to Islam for the souls of man, went unnoticed by most who entered the Dome. The man in the gold jacket wasn't bothered by trivialities as he slipped his shoes off to enter. His people's history was one made up of distorted details.

The Dome of the Rock was so named because it housed the 'Foundation Rock'. It was here that Mohammed rose to heaven during his infamous 'Night Journey'. Lesser so, but still with a place in Islam, was the Tradition also held that upon the same humongous stone, with its scuffs and imprints of time, Abraham had brought Isaac to be sacrificed before being prevented from doing so by an angel.

Jews claimed that the Rock actually marked where the Holies of Holies had been located inside Solomon's Temple but the man in the gold jacket dismissed this as propaganda. It was an excuse for the Jews to try and seize the Temple Mount and raze the Islamic structures on it.

Even if there were kernels of truth about the Jewish Temple being in this location, the man calculated there was no merit for honoring that fact now. History had seen to that. Like property rights from 1948, the spoils of war combined with the passage of time to change the dynamics on the ground. No, this was an Islamic site and would remain so. Allah would help his people see to that.

Dr. Ali Zarouk hadn't always held hardline beliefs. He was the last in a family of eight from Nazareth. His sister had been shot down while coming home from school. A protest had turned violent and the bullet that killed her had been a ricochet. A detail that served little consolation for the fact she was gone.

After that, Ali transitioned into a more religious lifestyle which in this land automatically meant being more political. When he rode the bus through Jerusalem, he winced every time he passed the bank headquartered on land his family had been forced to abandon in 1948 when they first fled to Nazareth. What was that bank and land worth now? Someone else had extracted their fortune off his family's misery.

Living in Yafo now where he worked, he couldn't always make it to Jerusalem. He had a good job at the Wolffsohn hospital. Holding Israeli citizenship, he was able to prosper better than most Palestinians especially the ones in the territories. He had economic opportunity and he had been successful in carefully walking the tightrope required in not allowing politics to derail his career.

The trip to the Temple Mount was a pilgrimage he made three or four times a year though and upon leaving the Dome of the Rock, he strolled to the nearby Al-Asqua Mosque. Once home to a crusader castle, the structure was a model of modesty when compared to the Dome of the Rock. The mosque was the third holiest site in Islam but in history probably more famous for being the place where King Abdullah I was gunned down.

All that was a detached history to Ali as he kneeled down on the designer rug facing Mecca to begin praying. What he was concerned with was the troubles of today and he had faith Allah would hear his pleas.

. . . .

JOHN 5:

[1] After this there was a feast of the Jews, and Jesus went up to Jerusalem. [2] Now there is in Jerusalem by the Sheep *Gate* a pool, which is called in Hebrew, Bethesda,[a] having five porches. [3] In these lay a great multitude of sick people, blind, lame, paralyzed, waiting for the moving of the water. [4] For an angel went down at a certain time into the pool and stirred up the water; then whoever stepped in first, after the stirring of the water, was made well of whatever disease he had.[b] [5] Now a certain man was there who had an infirmity thirty-eight years. [6] When Jesus saw him lying there, and knew that he already had been *in that condition* a long time, He said to him, "Do you want to be made well?"

[7] The sick man answered Him, "Sir, I have no man to put me into the pool when the water is stirred up; but while I am coming, another steps down before me."

[8] Jesus said to him, "Rise, take up your bed and walk." [9] And immediately the man was made well, took up his bed, and walked.

While Yossi paid the African nun at the ticket window for their entry fee, Lihi asked, "What is this place?"

Desica once again settled into her role as tour guide. "Well, the church, standing over there is St. Anne's."

She continued, "Those ruins over there are of Crusader-style church and where the pool of Bethesda was located." She took a little more time to delve into an explanation about the pool of Bethesda.

There was a pause inside the Church of St. Anne as the trio let their eyes adjust to the darker atmosphere. The smell of incense floated into their nostrils from candles lit near a statue in the rear of the building representing the Virgin Mary. Lihi let out a slight sneeze then smiled from embarrassment.

Their ears made adjustments as well as they tuned into the pleasant sounds of a group of English tourists who near the front altar had stopped long enough to render up hymns. The acoustics of the Church made their average Joe voices angelic as the chorus lifted to the stone ceiling. A crowd gathered behind them listening to the impromptu concert.

Back outside, Yossi peered down into the ruins that had once housed the pools of healing. Here hundreds had waited, vying for a chance to be first into the water. The healing waters were a lottery ticket and for every winner,

Yossi wondered how many losers there'd been. How many lives were wasted where he was standing, laying in wait for an opportunity that never arrived? Was there a point to such a system or was the universe meant to be so randomly skewed?

"Who was Serapis?" Desica asked. "It says here, there was a temple to Serapis on the grounds at some point."

"A popular Egyptian and Greek god that was often associated with healing," Yossi told her.

Desica's eyebrows rose slightly. "And you know this how?"

"We had to study it in college, an overview of mythology anyway," Yossi explained.

"Why?"

Resorting to memories of school days he hadn't recalled in a long time, Yossi rattled off, "I swear by Apollo, the healer, Asclepius, Hygieia, and Panacea, and I take to witness all the gods, all the goddesses, to keep according to my ability and my judgment, the following Oath and agreement: To consider dear to me, as my parents, him who taught me this art; to live in common with him and, if necessary, to share my goods with him; To look upon his children as my own brothers, to teach them this art. I will prescribe regimens for the good of my patients according to

my ability and my judgment and never do harm to anyone."
Yossi stopped there as Desica and Lihi stood in stunned
amazement.

"It's the opening of the original Hippocratic oath. Every
medical professional has to memorize it. Well, everyone
memorizes the modern one that's based on it anyway. Back
then they swore an oath of healing to the gods they knew.
Now days we pray to the one we know and put our patients
first and do no harm to anyone, at least when we can,"
Yossi explained.

For a moment a fresh image of those limbs piled up
outside the tent in Haiti rushed to the forefront of his mind.
Sometimes doing no harm wasn't an option.

"So, I guess it makes sense that they'd build a temple
here, a site that was based on healing," Desica concluded.

"I guess so," Yossi said his voice trailing off.

"They built churches here over the temple later, right?"
Lihi asked.

"Yeah," Desica answered, wondering where Yossi's
mind was floating off to this time.

The mystery veiling his personality was intriguing to her.
She couldn't help it. Maybe it was just the not knowing that
little kid instinct that says look in the closet even after your
parents tell you not too. Yossi had a very dark closet he

was keeping the door shut on and the temptation to pry was proving difficult to resist.

"Come on, let's walk down into the ruins," Lihi suggested.

The girls went on ahead but Yossi leaned against the railing, towering over the history that formed this place. Where was the pool for him to find his own healing? Who'd stitch up the lingering wounds?

.   .   .   .   .   .

The first sister could still feel the misery haunting the pools by the arched porches, the desperation of those who'd lain helpless waiting for waters to be stirred. People who clung to the faith believed there was a hope, a chance for them to be touched. They struggled every waking hour to keep their faith whole.

FAITH, where was righteousness without it? What kind of future lay on the horizon in its absence? While waiting for an angel you might find a Jesus instead but not without faith.

Yossi felt a chill up his back. Goosebumps popped up on his arm and he shuddered from the sudden sensation which had come out of nowhere.

121

A female voice whispered, "What do you see in those ruins? Do you think it was the water that healed the ill?"

Yossi spun around but he was standing alone against the rail. A tour group was a few yards away and the girls had already started descending the steps toward what had been the main floor of the Byzantium era Church.

Glancing down into the pit, he heard the voice again, "Oh, ye of little faith."

"But I have faith." Yossi startled himself by answering out loud. A nearby lady in a yellow floppy hat stared at him strangely.

"The people that lay here had no one to help. They were alone. You are not. Help yourself or drown not in the waters of healing but in the sorrows of self-pity," the voice cautioned him.

Yossi waited for more but the voice went silent.

.   .   .   .

"There you are," Desica declared as Yossi joined them in what had probably been the sanctuary of a Crusader church.

"Sorry, I was looking at something up top," Yossi lied rather unconvincingly.

Lihi was busy punching the keys on her cell phone.

"You have to go?" Desica asked her.

"Nah. He's running late," Lihi replied.

"What's new, right?" The two girls laughed.

"My boyfriend, Naftali, is always late. Always," Lihi said dismissively.

"Do you know what I want to do?" Desica asked while tugging Lihi along to show her.

The two climbed up on some rocky stair like formation and hoisted themselves up onto an arch that had been standing for centuries. Yossi, raised his camera and snapped a photo.

The girls sat down on the archway. Desica leaned over and whispered to Lihi who nodded mischievously her agreement.

"Get your camera ready," Desica warned.

"Ok." Yossi was prepared to shoot the photo but wasn't sure of what.

The girls sat down on the beam-like archway. Lihi slid her rifle off and laid it within arm's reach. Then as Desica counted to three, the two girls leaned backward, almost upside down, with their legs clutching the archway so they wouldn't fall on their heads.

"Ok, take the picture!" Desica shouted as her glasses fell off her face and onto the ground.

As he shot the photo, Yossi noticed Desica's big blue eyes which he'd only gotten a glimpse of back at the café.

"I bet the crusaders didn't dream of someone ever doing this," Desica declared as the girls struggled to pull themselves back up. Lihi almost slipped and Yossi darted over to catch her but she caught herself before she actually fell.

As the girls climbed down to ground-level again, Lihi's phone signaled another text message. This time she had to leave to wait at a bus stop for the ever elusive Naftali.

"I guess I should go too," Desica stated as a group of tourists descended down into the church ruins with a tour guide reciting a well-practiced spiel explaining the historical significance of the archaeological find.

"Ok. I'm glad you came over to my table though," Yossi told her.

She smiled. "Me, too. Someday, you'll have to tell me what you were thinking about at that moment."

"Someday," he agreed.

"Do you have your phone?" she asked.

Yossi pulled it out.

"Here, dial this number, 0526433225," she instructed.

He complied and suddenly Desica's phone began playing Madonna's 'Hung Up'. "Now we have each other's number. Call me some time." She said before putting her sunglasses back on, turning around, and walking back up the stairs to leave.

"Yeah, I'll do that," Yossi said only to see in the corner of his eye the same lady with the yellow floppy hat starring at him rather intensely.

CHAPTER 7: The Dock

"What time do you have?" the man with a slight scar under his left eye asked Lady Marina with a raised voice overriding the techno blaring in the pizza parlor where they were sitting.

Lady Marina glanced down at her blue watch. "We're on schedule."

"We can't be late," the man reminded her in a heavy Russian accent.

"Don't worry, Guy. We'll make it," Marina assured him.

Guy motioned for the waiter to bring him the bill. "I really like this place."

Poco's was a quaint, to the point of being placed in the category of trendy, pizzeria on the corner of Herzl and Rothschild in Tel Aviv. The crowd skewed younger but it had a down to earth feel to the atmosphere.

"The pizza is really good too," Lady Marina added.

"Why do you think I suggested it?" Guy asked with a smirk before throwing his money down on the table.

This intersection was the birthplace of Tel Aviv, the place where it all started and where the city still bustled. The Hall of Independence where David Ben-Gurion had announced the creation of the Jewish State of Israel to a worldwide

126

audience and thousands lining Rothschild was only a block away. One of the first houses in Tel Aviv, if not the very first one, was cattycorner to Poco's.

Lady Marina and Guy Brezhnev weaved through the throngs of people milling about the neighborhood on what was a typical clear-sky night. In Tel Aviv, the moonlight is only lost in the city lights.

Young couples crowded the string of cafes lining the boulevards. The sounds of laughter mixed readily with a music laden background. Pet owners in shorts and sandals kept their animals tightly leashed so as not to bother other pedestrians on the narrow sidewalks. Occasionally, the pets stopped their owners long enough to get acquainted with each other before being yanked along again.

The setting was a picturesque scene opposite the dark disturbing desperation Lady Marina had fled in Addis Ababa. Here there was life and a feeling of anticipation which she thrived on. In Addis Ababa, the sensation had been more of a prisoner trapped by circumstance wondering if she'd ever escape.

Escape she had although she wasn't all the way back home to the Ukraine yet. The organization which employed her had offered her a chance to relocate to Israel and oversee their dealings on the docks for them. How could

127

she say, no? She couldn't if she wanted to see another sunrise. That was the whole point.

The occupational risks were greater in Israel than in Ethiopia. In Ethiopia, smuggling mainly consisted of negotiating the bribe amount with the right person. As long as the price was agreed too, things got done. Relatively speaking, free trade flourished.

In Israel, money changed hands but if something went wrong, a shipment got intercepted, or an operative was arrested, then those paid off were guaranteed to run for cover in an effort to save their own skins.

Over a million Russians, Ukrainians, and Eastern Europeans had made 'aliya' – immigration – to Israel since the 1900s. With them came the old ways including the crime syndicates who'd prevailed even under the Iron Curtain. The community was still tight knit, speaking Russian as often as Hebrew for instance, but while there was safety in numbers, in Marina's line of business, it was far from being the shield of invincibility.

She looked over at Guy who grinned at her as they climbed into the jeep. As a teenager, he was part of that giant aliya and had been raised in Bat Yam just south of Tel Aviv. He was Israeli but his Russian characteristics surfaced like a birthright not to be shaken off.

Marina started the jeep wondering when the next time she'd see Guy would be. It was a casual arrangement between them. She couldn't demand more and counted herself lucky to see him at all. There was also the age difference; he being years younger than her but when they were together it didn't seem to matter.

Still, there was a portion of her heart that desired more though maybe not necessarily with Guy. That might not be reasonable to expect. With his flat dark hair, and tall, lean body accented by the muscles he'd formed from the daily visit to the weight trainer, he could pretty well land any lady in Tel Aviv he wanted. Still, Guy's presence had resurfaced memories of how much she'd been attached to her late husband. Whatever flaws her deceased husband possessed, the love between them had been real. She longed for that sense of belonging once again.

Marina questioned whether she was setting herself up for a fall. After all, while she'd loved her husband, he had betrayed her by ripping off his business partners and destroying her life. It's what got him killed.

Was she letting her feelings about Guy blind her to his true nature? Would she in the end, find herself picking up the pieces of a disastrous end? Maybe next time it'd be her body being dumped in a canal.

Weaving in and out of the Tel Aviv traffic, Marina avoided vehicles and pedestrians alike as she sped toward the Yafo docks, only a 15-minute drive from where they'd been eating pizza.

The driver of the number 25 bus was singing to himself and struggling to stay in tune, a task made slightly easier by the radio playing Leonard Cohen songs. A local station was doing 30 straight minutes of the artist and the driver knew all of Cohen's lyrical poetry by memory. The double-length bus was stacked with commuters headed in the direction of the working neighborhoods of Yafo and Bat Yam.

He looked into his mirror, fixating briefly on a rail of a teenage girl with a Milla Jovovich face dressed in a green T-shirt that showed soaked spots in the back because her hair was of still wet hair. Maybe she'd spent the evening at the sea shore. The older guy she was with had an array of piercings and a cropped mohawk. As she put her arm around Mr. Punk Rocker, the driver speculated on what it was like to be young again. Would he have had the guts to sport a mohawk? His mother would've killed him. A low laugh sent Leonard Cohen's words even further off key.

As the bus entered the traffic circle near the famous Clock Tower marking the heart of old Yafo, the lyrics stopped as the driver laid on the horn.

130

The air brakes let loose a 'whoosh.'

Lady Marina treated the horn as background noise, squeezing between the bus and two motorcycles who split wide enough to create a space for her jeep to dart through. She yanked hard on the wheel sending the jeep careening across other traffic trying to navigate the intersection in an orderly fashion.

The Passengers on the bus gripped to railings and seats for dear life as their bodies lurched about like a ball caught between two flappers in a pinball machine. The girl in the green shirt started falling over but her adored mohowk friend caught her which earned him an appreciative inviting smile.

As the bus driver watched Lady Marina speed away, he wished to himself the bus had been empty so he could've plowed her under. The jeep was no match for the massive vehicle of steel whose helm he sat behind. He looked up; everyone on the bus was fine even though swear words were being uttered. He put the vehicle in gear and started back down the route.

The Yafo docks were deserted this time of night. The two guards standing watch were taking a 'break' as had been pre-arranged so Lady Marina sped past the guard shack, took a sharp turn, and headed down a narrow street where ancient buildings housed private warehouses.

Slowing to a stop in front of a small iron door that fronted a stone building, Lady Marina could hear the incoming tide sending waves crashing against the breakwall. In the night air, the splashing actually made a soothing sound that calmed Lady Marina.

The full history of these docks would never be documented. In use for thousands of years, the port of Yafo had seen its share of merchants and conquerors set anchor here.

Out in the bay, the Rock of Andromeda sat, so named after the daughter of the Queen of Ethiopia who had dared to brag her daughter was more beautiful than the off-spring of a god, only to have the god torment her kingdom with a monster. As punishment, the queen had to chain her daughter to the rock to be sacrificed to the sea monster. But struck by Andromeda's beauty, the returning Perseus, fresh from his victory over Medusa, rescued her and married her. They founded a dynasty that ruled the Kingdom of Mycenae. At times, Lady Marina felt like she'd been strapped to a rock for similar purposes only in her case a Perseus hadn't bothered to stop.

Lady Marina caught a glimpse of her forearm. The dye from the new tattoo reflected in the moonlight. The falcon looked pretty cool she thought. She really had to quit getting tattoos or in another decade she'd be covered head to foot like a co-worker she once knew who had ended up disappearing in the Burmese jungle.

Guy held up his watch to get a better view. The Tel Aviv skyline, with its skyscrapers, lit up the nighttime from a distance.

The roar of a diesel engine gravitated their attention back to the current situation. A cargo truck slowed on approach before switching off its headlights.

Guy greeted a person who jumped out from the passenger side. They quietly exchanged a few words before the passenger went to the back and opened up the cargo area.

Guy motioned for Lady Marina who met him at the iron warehouse door.

"Yuri said to give these guys whatever they want and to leave what they don't. Understand?" Guy asked.

"Sure. Let them take what they want." Lady Marina was a little perplexed. There was no need to repeat the instructions. What was she, a newbie?

Guy tossed her the keys. Lady Marina opened up the rusty lock and the rust on the doors squeaked as she swung them open.

"It's your pick," Guy told their contact.

Marina flipped on a flashlight as the group entered. Uncharacteristically, she let out a small gasp of disgust.

"Remember, Yuri said they take what they want. No questions asked." Guy repeated.

What had caused Lady Marina's gasp wasn't the boxes of black market goods. Those were an everyday occurrence and she probably would've been really scared if they hadn't been there. No, what caught her attention this night was the cargo, for lack of a better term, next to the boxes stenciled with Chinese lettering.

Forced to sit on the ground because they were chained to an overweight crate, were three women of various nationalities. Their hands and legs were bound by the chain which used their own weight as a further determent.

Lady Marina could see their mouths were taped. Muffled sounds and grunts were barely audible as the prisoners pleaded for relief. Lady Marina could tell they'd been abandoned there for at least a day and were dirty, hungry and squirming in their own filth.

Human cargo wasn't Lady Marina's normal forte but she wasn't in a position to cross Yuri. Besides, she was only there to backup Guy should the deal go south. Open the door, watch his back, then get off the dock as quickly as possible.

She watched as the person from the truck came over and examined the three women. He loosened the first two and yanked them up but the third he shook his head at and left her chained.

"This one's sick," he informed them.

Having reached wits-end in the darkened warehouse prison, the third woman begged through the tape to also be taken even knowing the fate wasn't pleasant. The man ignored her.

"I'm not paying for damaged merchandise," the contact declared.

"Fine. We'll subtract it from your tab," Guy offered.

In a few moments after boxes were loaded up and the two girls being transported were securely hidden in the back of the truck, Lady Marina reached for the door. She caught a vague glimpse of the darkened shadow being left as the door swung shut.

Lady Marina could've lied and told her it'd be ok. But she knew - the two of them both knew - that wasn't going

135

to be the case. Lady Marina guess was the human cargo would be at the bottom of the Mediterranean in about 48 hours.

"I'm going with them," Guy informed Lady Marina as she replaced the lock back onto the door.

"What?" This wasn't the plan at all.

"They need a hand and there is still some money to be exchanged," Guy explained.

"But ..." Lady Marina started.

"What's the big deal? Are you worried about me?" Guy asked.

"Would I waste my time?" Lady Marina shot back.

"Not the Lady Marina, I know," he answered.

"I just don't like last minute changes in the plans that's all. It's bad business and creates unnecessary risk."

"Normally, I'd agree but I think I need to baby-sit the cargo until the payment is in hand," Guy reasoned.

Lady Marina relented, "Ok."

"Call you next week?"

"If you wish," Lady Marina was curt in her invitation.

Guy hopped into the truck and Lady Marina watched as it drove off to a destination she had no privy too. Sometimes, ignorance was a life insurance policy in her line of work.

She hopped into her own jeep. The gears cranked up as she took off, as a safety precaution, in a different direction. As she rounded a corner near Andromeda Hill, her headlights froze three Haredim in their tracks. She slammed on the brakes.

The Haredim were up to ill-conceived destruction. Lady Marina instantly realized that. Very few of the Ultra-Orthodox Jews actually lived in Yafo. When they came here it was to destroy an object of their disdain under the cover of darkness. Occasionally, a large rally of them protested in broad daylight so others could see how much they valued their self-worth.

The Haredim, who as a community had by choice not progressed any further than the 19th century, displayed a tendency to vandalize archaeological sites in the area. Lady Marina suspected this group was up to doing precisely that but she decided to let them pass unabated. She didn't desire any entanglements coming off the docks after a job.

Bam was the metal sound her hood made as one of the Haredim slammed his fist down on it.

Lady Marina turned off the jeep and jumped out. The first Haredi was saying something about a woman's proper place this time of night when Lady Marina sent him to the ground with a good right cross. A follow-up kick to the groin kept him there.

The thing about the Haredim is they aren't in great shape. The other two were still looking stunned from the fact a woman was attacking them when Lady Marina used another kick to take the knees out of the second one.

The third one, more used to throwing stones from a distance than actually engaging in hand to hand combat, threw a punch which Lady Marina easily ducked. Grabbing her opponent's wrist, Lady Marina pulled his arm back, reached for his fingers, and with a yank from her other hand bent two fingers back until she heard a snap followed by a cry of pain.

Lesson learned Lady Marina figured as she turned the man loose. She watched as the wounded gathered themselves before making a dash for safety.

She was almost back in the jeep when a noise from a nearby alley caught her attention. Lady Marina hesitated for a moment debating whether to investigate. It could be more Haredim, hiding after what they saw happen to the first group. Suddenly, a small wail rang out.

Lady Marina tried convincing herself it was one of the thousands of stray cats roaming Yafo but a second cry nixed that notion and Lady Marina, not wanting to leave anything to chance, decided it was best to venture down the dark alley.

Cautiously, she approached. The noise originated near a shop that was obviously closed. Specifically, the cry, which was persistent now, came from behind a stack of boxes.

Lady Marina scanned her surroundings. No one else was within sight although she knew if she didn't hurry that would soon change. She moved a couple of the boxes until she reached a pile of rubbish where she found a carved out plastic wastebasket serving as a crib. Inside the homemade crib was a small baby wrapped in a worn blue blanket.

The baby girl, as it turned out to be, stopped crying long enough to give Lady Marina the once over, smile then resume the cry. Lady Marina could tell the kid was hungry, and after a check discovered a diaper change was in order as well.

She debated with herself. Where would she keep the kid? She could drop him off at the authorities but they might ask where the baby was found and under no circumstances could Lady Marina divulge that she was on the dock this evening.

Another sound caught Lady Marina's ear. This one was more familiar from her time on the docks. Rats. Those flea invested pestilent creatures that were a bane to all mankind as attested to by anyone who survived the Black Death. Eventually, Lady Marina knew they'd make their way to the baby.

Grabbing the child, she briskly walked to the jeep, setting the makeshift crib down in the floorboard where it'd be safer and out of sight from the roaming eyes of traffic cops.

Pressing in on the clutch, she looked down and said, "Hang on kid. You're going for a ride."

.   .   .   .

Back at the building housing her flat, Lady Marina quickly carried the child upstairs undetected. She set the basket down on the kitchen table and stared at it as though the longer she examined it the more likely a solution was to pop into her mind.

Lady Marina opened her fridge. Half a liter of water, a couple swallows of soda, a rotting tomato, and a single egg was all the shelves held, none of it exactly of interest to a toddler.

Leaving verbal instructions for the kid to sit still, Lady Marina left her second floor flat and jogged back down to the first apartment where she rapidly knocked on the door.

The Filipino answering the door in her pink robe, seemed irritated from the get go at having been woken up. "What do you want?"

"I need you to come upstairs," Lady Marina said.

"At this hour? I have to work in the morning. What time is it anyway?" The Filipino looked down at her watch.

"Please?"

"Look at the time!" The Filipino held up her Casio watch in case Lady Marina didn't believe her.

Lady Marina's face took a measure of sternness as she said, "I insist."

The Filipino didn't know Lady Marina well. After all, Lady Marina wasn't exactly normally sociable. But everyone in the building knew she was connected with people you didn't want to cross so the Filipino lady shrugged and reluctantly followed Lady Marina to her flat.

The Filipino lady's eyes lit up at the sight and sounds of the baby.

"Oh, it's so cute!" she cooed.

"Is it yours? Of course not," the Filipino said answering her own question.

"Look, you're a nurse and its crying."

"Babies do that." The Filipino suspected she was seeing a rare glimpse of vulnerability in Lady Marina.

"I know. I know. But, it is hungry, needs a diaper change, and I thought you might have some of those things," Lady Marina stated.

"I take care of an old lady who gets around on a walker when she gets around at all," the nurse explained.

"I have to do something. *We* have to do something," Lady Marina insisted.

"The authorities?"

Lady Marina shook her head.

"Let me borrow your cell," the nurse requested.

"Why?" Lady Marina asked.

"Why do you think? You want my help? Then lend me your phone," the nurse demanded.

Lady Marina parted with the phone and watched as the nurse made a call to a second nurse. The Filipino stayed and played with the baby until a deliveryman arrived with a box of goods containing formula, diapers and a bib.

"These will get you started. Go tomorrow and buy more supplies, you hear?" the nurse instructed.

"I will," Lady Marina promised.

Grabbing a pen, the nurse wrote down a number. "You can reach me here if you have questions about what to do, ok?"

Lady Marina acknowledged that she understood.

"Good luck," the nurse said upon leaving the flat.

Closing the door, Lady Marina returned to the kitchen table. She looked at the baby, then the box of goods, then the baby again. It was going to be a long, long, night.

CHAPTER 8: Tourists & Immigrants Pt. 1

"Those are so cool." Cole was staring up at a sky filled with a rainbow of kites of elaborately crafted designs, zigzagging amongst each other, their tails fluttering in the warm breeze. A mixture of kids and adults were pulling at the strings trying to keep them afloat.

"Oh, Eric would have a field day if he was here," Monique stated wistfully.

"Wouldn't he though," Cole concurred.

Monique scanned the sandy shoreline draped in the background by the Mediterranean Sea. In this tourist hot spot, magnificent ruins from a once thriving metropolis slumbered in the sand. She'd never been here before and that was what was nagging at her. She knew exactly where the amphitheatre was supposed to be located and how the rest of the aqueduct, collapsed by time, was suppose to run. The feeling was a cross between de je vu and an old home movie you hadn't seen in awhile.

"You want to go look at the Crusader fortifications?" Cole asked.

Monique rolled her eyes, "You promised me!"

Cole defended himself. "What? I didn't say I wouldn't look at *any*. Besides, we're here, we might as well take a peek around Caesarea and see what it used to be like."

"You never just take a peek. Besides, I have a good sense what it used to be like already," Monique concluded. "Tell you what, sweetheart, why don't you go take a look at the fortifications and I will join you shortly, ok?"

"What are you going to do?" Cole asked.

Monique pointed the opposite way. "I want to walk over in that direction."

"You sure?"

"I'm a big girl. I'll be ok," Monique teased.

Cole shrugged, "all right."

The pair split up with Cole trotting over to join others from the tour group who'd already made their way to the ancient fortifications while Monique followed her instinct to an area not far off.

. . . .

"Cute baby," Monique complimented a lady pacing about near her though it wasn't the baby's looks that garnered Monique's attention, but rather the lady's tattoos.

"Thank you," the lady acknowledged in broken English. Her dark glasses shielded her eyes, and a ball cap blocked the summer sun from the rest of her face.

"Is it a boy or girl?" Monique asked while making googly eyes at the baby.

"Girl," Lady Marina replied.

"Well, you look good for someone who just had a baby," Monique remarked.

"You see „. "

Monique, realizing she may have assumed too much, interrupted the lady, "It is yours, right?"

Lady Marina, growing increasingly annoyed, reluctantly answered, "Yes, yes it is. Thank you for the compliment."

"What's her name?" Monique asked.

"What?"

"The baby's name? She does have a name right?" Monique chuckled.

A name? A name? No one had asked Lady Marina this question before now and she hadn't given much consideration to the fact the baby needed a name. Why hadn't this occurred to her before now? What if it had been a police officer asking her these questions instead of some dingy American tourist?

"I'm sorry, I didn't mean to pry." Monique backed off.

"No, no, it is ok," Lady Marina said.

"The baby's name is … " Lady Marina looked down at the baby while Monique waited with anticipation, "the baby's name is Katrina," Lady Marina resolved.

"Katrina. That is a beautiful name," Monique said.

"It was my mother's," Lady Marina explained.

"What are you doing, here? Shouldn't you be over with the other tourists?" Lady Marina asked.

It was a good question for which Monique didn't have a great answer. "Probably, but I'm just looking around on my own for a bit."

"This area where we're standing use to be an inland harbor before they filled it in," Lady Marina explained.

Monique was surprised, "You know about the harbors here?"

"I like the water. It lets you go places. Even now, your mind can float out with the tide if you allow it," Lady Marina divulged.

"I never thought of it like that." Monique stated.

"I have, many times. Are you interested in the ancient harbor?" Lady Marina wondered.

"Not, particularly. Honestly, I don't know what I expected to find over here," Monique admitted.

Lady Marina said, "I say that only because you don't know what you're looking for. Another great thing about the ocean, you don't have to know. It lets you think, search, explore with the freedom to go anywhere you wish."

The answer struck a chord with Monique whose entire expression changed. That dream. She quickly glanced around to get her bearings, realizing the sensation of familiarity she'd be experiencing might not be so out of the norm after all.

Lady Marina saw the facial transformation on Monique. "Are you ok?"

"Yes, yes. I'm fine. A little too much sun, I suppose," Monique told her.

"Be careful. The sun will get the best of you if you're not careful," Lady Marina warned.

"Ah, there you are!" a man with a scar beneath his eye exclaimed loud enough to cause tourists within earshot to turn their heads.

"Hello," Lady Marina greeted the man who gave her a kiss on the lips in return.

"Who's this?" The man indicated Monique.

"I'll talk to you later. Nice chatting with you." Monique was aware she'd gone from curiosity seeker to just being intrusive.

Monique quickly did an about face and walked away.

The man repeated his question, "Who was that?"

"Nobody. A tourist."

"Whose baby is that?"

"Mine," Lady Marina declared.

"Yours? *Yours*?"

"It is possible you know," Lady Marina replied.

"Maybe so, but not in under nine months and why here? Why drag it all the way out here?" Irritation laced Guy's tone.

"I don't know any babysitters, ok? There. She's here because I had no place else to take her. Besides, it's good cover. Who is going to suspect a lady holding her baby? Huh?" Marina smirked then smiled at the baby.

"This is so no good," Guy stated.

"Guy, meet Katrina. Katrina, this is Guy. He's a heartbreaker who is put off by babies so be careful around him." Katrina gave a smile then blew a bubble from her mouth.

.   .   .   .

Monique surveyed her surroundings. There were just enough of the ancient ruins to help recall the dream. "Let's see. I met that guy about here. No, wait, it was more over this way. Yeah that's it."

She knew she looked crazy to anyone passing her but somehow talking aloud and answering herself reassured her that she wasn't. Hearing the facts as she remembered them made that elusive state seem clearer.

"Then we walked this way and turned a corner." Her reenactment brought forth no answers even though she vividly recalled doing these things.

Monique stopped and looked ahead. There were tourists milling about. Locals enjoying the scenery of another beautiful day and workers eking a living off the tourist trade, but there were no ancient dwellings standing. No visitors coming off the dock. No Roman soldiers double-timing it to carry out the Prefect's orders. All that lay in front of her was wasteland and ruins. Even if she knew the exact number of steps she'd taken in the dream and so she retraced them but it still led her nowhere because the 'where' didn't exist any longer. Monique sighed. It was a shame. She'd like to have seen that guy and his daughters again.

"Hey!"

Monique turned to see Cole approaching.

"I thought you were going to meet me," he said.

"I was just going that way. I wanted a few minutes to myself to explore something," she told him.

Cole looked around. "Explore what?"

"Turns out it was nothing," she replied, enticing a mystified look from Cole.

"I did meet an interesting woman," Monique glanced back where she'd bumped into Marina only to see her and the man had vanished.

"Where is she at?" Cole asked.

"Gone now, I suppose. She was carrying the cutest baby. It was adorable."

"What was the lady's name?" Cole inquired.

"You know, I never asked. The baby's name though was Katrina. It was adorable."

There was an awkward pause as Monique had a rather serious brainstorm. "Have you ever thought about us having another one?"

Cole was flabbergasted by the salvo shot out of nowhere.

"No, not really," he timidly answered.

"I was just wondering," she explained.

"Have you? Thought about it that is?" Cole asked.

"Not until just this moment." Monique shuffled past Cole to rejoin the tour group.

CHAPTER 9: Two Gardens

Monique sat on the bench, her back leaning against a church building. She peered through the iron fencing in front of her that had been erected to protect a grove of Olive Trees which had stood their ground for countless centuries. Even now, this grove was amazingly withstanding the onslaught of pilgrims flocking to this once calm corner of Jerusalem.

It had to have been peaceful, Monique reasoned, because this is where Jesus came to find solace in his darkest hour. The garden was a place where introspective examination was encouraged. This locale, the Garden of Gethsemane, had once upon a time literally been the calm before the storm.

That was eons ago when the only interruption a radical upstart had to worry about was the guards coming to haul you away. It was so peaceful here, back then that even the disciples had managed to set aside their worries and fall asleep.

Monique had roamed the garden trying to find an isolated place where she could collect her thoughts so she found a bench next to the trees to sit on as people filed past.

She'd surprised Cole with her initial reaction about the baby. It hadn't been her intention to do that and for the life of her, she couldn't figure out where that response sprung forth. Cole deserved better but at the moment her emotions were a wild pendulum swinging side to side out of control. She'd hoped for a respite in the Garden given its history but unlike Jesus, she couldn't even say a prayer to herself.

Turns out there was no peace in the garden with the pilgrims from Brazil rampaging about, or the Baptists from Alabama who were slipping samples of soil into their pockets. With all the groups milling around the grounds there was little chance for serious self-reflection.

The Church of the Agony, or Church of All Nations as it was also known, had been built in the garden. It was one of several churches dotting the Mount of Olives landscape, erected by rulers and the religious hierarchy to prove their loyalty to the faith.

Monique didn't know if it was a reflection of her Catholic upbringing, but she'd become immune on this trip to seeing churches built as holy markers over every rock, twig, and pothole where biblical figures once stopped to stare at a star. Somehow the gaudiness of it all overwhelmed the simplicity the faith was rooted upon.

The art work inside the churches was often amazing. In the Church of All Nations, the painter had captured the spirit with his depiction overlooking the altar. It just was hard to enjoy or appreciate with a thousand cameras running or as Monique had witnessed, a lady laying prostate upon the rock at the altar as though somehow the energy from the rock boosted her righteousness.

"Glad to see you're having a good time." Cole slid onto the bench next to Monique.

"I had forgotten how much a circus these tourist spots can be," Monique told him.

"It is a bit much isn't it," Cole agreed.

"I think I need some beach time, *soon*."

"And you'll get it. I promise," Cole assured her.

"You gonna lay out in the sun with me?" Monique asked in a suggestive fashion.

"How could I pass up an invitation like that?" Cole leaned over and gave her a kiss.

"Listen, about the comment I made yesterday ..." Monique started.

"Cole did you see this view? I tell you, this is so magnificent," the voice of Sis. Gladys rang out above the din in the garden.

"Later," Cole mouthed to Monique.

154

Sis. Gladys tugged at Cole's arm. "You have to take a look at this. You too, Monique."

"Oh, I'm good," Monique assured Sis. Gladys. Monique watched as Cole was reluctantly dragged to the edge of the garden for a view of the Old City from a perspective that Cole had already seen.

Monique tilted her head back. Though the skies were clear she could see nothing. How was she to find what she needed on this trip? She may not know what she was looking for but she definitely could tell you what she wasn't seeking and this was it.

She glanced around at the lines of people and the jabberwocky going on. Yep, if Jesus were here, he wouldn't find solace, he'd lose his mind, she concluded.

Over by the edge of the Garden, Sis. Gladys was busy showing Cole the view of the Old City from the Mount Olives. The ancient walls and the golden Dome of the Rock looked majestic from across the valley.

"Just breathtaking," Sis. Gladys repeated.

"I suppose it is," Cole conceded.

"I'm glad you think so," Rev. Hasbro interrupted. "Cole this is Avi."

Avi reached out to shake Cole's hand, "Nice to meet you."

"Likewise," Cole politely said while not having an inclination who the official looking Israeli with the designer sunglasses was.

"Avi is with the Israeli Film Office," Rev. Hasbro explained. Sis. Gladys had forgotten about the magnificent view and had refocused on the conversation.

"Excuse us," Rev. Hasbro said and motioned for the men to follow him a few steps.

"I understand you are interested in filming a television show," Avi said to Cole.

"I guess that is the case," Cole responded.

"Well, Israel can offer you a lot. How many other locales offer you a historic view like this to put into your shot? It is a religious show, yes?" Avi asked.

"Yes," Cole answered.

"Well, what will boost your ratings more than filming where Jesus stood?" Avi pointed out.

"George Washington slept here," Cole quipped.

The reference was lost on Avi, "What?"

"Nothing. A bad American joke. Yes, the view is marvelous but will we be able to do what we want to do? As Shakespeare put it, 'This is the question'." Cole responded.

Avi kept the sales pitch going, "A lot of big Christian talk hosts come here and do their shows. There is a hotel down the road that many of them use as a place to set up."

"Yeah, I know but we're not interested in another boring talk show," Cole explained.

"Tell me more about the show and let me see how I can help you," Avi countered.

Cole outlined the concept, "We want to film what it is for people of our faith, probably young people, to leave their homes and journey to a place like Israel where they can practice and help others. We would film their struggles and their experiences."

"I see." Avi had a concerned expression on his face.

"Does that present a problem?" Rev. Hasbro asked.

"Maybe. We don't allow any proselytizng. Your people won't be able to come here and attempt to convert anyone to your religion." Avi explained.

"But you just said Christian talk show hosts film here all the time," Rev. Hasbro hadn't anticipated this obstacle.

"Yes, but talking to other people of the same faith on a show that will be shown in another country is different from going out and trying to recruit new converts on our streets," Avi pointed out.

"I don't know where that leaves us then," Rev. Hasbro concluded.

"You have other churches, modern churches that exist here, right?" Cole asked.

"Of course. We accept people of all religions just as long as they don't try to convert people," Avi stressed.

"But our people could work in the ministries of these churches without problems, right?" Cole asked.

"Yes, that would be acceptable." Avi thought he knew where Cole was going with this line of thought.

"And we could film the participants reactions to visiting the Holy sites around the country," Cole surmised.

Rev. Hasbro agreed, "Yes that might be worth watching."

"The Ministry of Tourism would have no problem with that," Avi stated.

"Well, let us see what we can work out on that basis then. I mean, the people back home will still have to approve," Cole told Avi.

"I understand but just keep in mind, trying to convert anyone is a criminal offense. If they accept that then Israel will welcome you with open arms. I will leave you then. You have my number if you need more information." Avi left Rev. Hasbro and Cole to mull over the new roughly developed concept for the show.

. . . .

"It does look like a skull," Monique observed.

"I don't see it. I just don't see it," Sis. Gladys remarked.

"Well, look. See the holes there in the side of the hill? Those are eyes," Cole pointed to the indentations in the hill that made it stand out from the others.

"Think of a pirate skull," Rev. Hasbro suggested.

"Yes, a pirate skull. You can see why Gen. Gordon would've thought this was the place. It fits the description perfectly," Cole declared.

"General who?" Rev. Hasbro asked.

Cole explained, "General Gordon. Also known as Chinese Gordon or Khartoum Gordon which was unfortunately a moniker he acquired when he was martyred in Khartoum during an Islamic jihad.

He was the English General who was standing on Jerusalem's Old City walls right over there, looked out, saw the skull features which is an interpretation of the word Golgotha, realized the hill was outside the city walls which the site of the crucifixion had to be, and went viola! That has to be the place."

Sis. Gladys leaned back from where she was standing on the observation deck at the Garden Tomb. Then she leaned further in on the railing as though trying to decide which angle gave her the better view.

"Well, I guess it does resemble a pirate skull. Maybe, General Gordon knew what he was talking about. What about the Church of the Holy Sepulcher? Isn't that suppose to be the spot also?" Sis. Gladys inquired.

A tour guide standing behind them chimed in on the discussion, "The Church was declared the spot of Jesus' crucifixion by the Empress Helene who was traveling through the land at the time specifically to designate religious spots. The truth is though, from a historical and archaeological perspective, it is unclear if the Church was outside the city walls when Jesus was alive. No one knows for sure."

"But there are so many churches and chapels, so many different religions inside the Church of the Holy Sepulcher," Sis. Gladys pointed out.

The tour guide answered, "True. But like I said, an Empress made it the holy spot and who is going to argue with an Empress?"

"What's that up there?" Monique pointed to the top of the hill.

"A Muslim cemetery," the tour guide answered. "It keeps non-believers off the top of the hill and also means there can be no exploration of the place."

"Imagine what they might find," Cole wondered aloud.

Sis. Gladys turned her nose up. "Who'd want to go digging around where there'd been a cemetery? That is morbid."

"It is what archaeologists do." Rev. Hasbro was exasperated by the lack of foresight in Sis. Gladys' reasoning.

"If that is where Jesus was crucified, who knows what artifacts might lay below the surface?" Cole said.

"I still think it is morbid," Sis. Gladys remarked.

"What's morbid is that down below." The group took their eyes off Golgotha and shifted their gaze below where bellows of exhaust fumes rose from the Arab East Jerusalem bus terminal, a lot, overcrowded with vehicles and people. Kids scampered from bus to bus with bags of candy they were selling.

"It does seem a little excessive," Cole agreed.

The group left the observation deck of the Garden Tomb and continued down one of its paths decorated with well kept plants and trees. The path led them to the actual tomb which was the center piece of the grounds.

The Garden Tomb, as it was popularly called, is located yards away from the Damascus Gate of the Old City of Jerusalem. A walled off plot of land, it is protected by a private English foundation whose sole purpose is its upkeep and to keep urban encroachment, like the bus station on the other side of the land boundary, at bay.

At the tomb itself, one of the Garden's guides, a retired gentleman from Kent who was spending half-a-year volunteering for the Foundation, explained the workings of a first century tomb. He relayed the story of the resurrection for reference. Tourists were pausing in front of the tomb which visitors had to duck to enter. After his brief presentation he invited everyone to enter to take a look.

On a typical Sunday morning behind the pulpit, Rev. Hasbro might have told his congregation, "This was the purpose of it all. This is one of the keys to being a Christian; the power of a rolled away stone."

That message resonated in Rev. Hasbro as he stepped through the narrow entrance that was the opening of the Garden Tomb, the very entrance where an angel had once greeted the female mourners coming to visit a deceased Jesus.

"Had it been worth it, though?" the clergyman wondered as he peered over a small fence that had been erected to protect the area where the body of Jesus had lain.

Lately, the good reverend had been experiencing unusual bouts of doubt. It wasn't a questioning of his faith as much as the path he'd chosen in pursuing that faith. On Sunday mornings when he peered out across the congregation sporting their Sunday best and singing hymns, he secretly wondered, had he made any inroads with his ministry?

The Sunday morning before they'd left for the trip, when congregants were busy speculating about the tour and those who couldn't go were expressing their envy of those who could, and many were sharing their fantasies of what it was going to be like, Rev. Hasbro was busy engaging in a flurry of speculation.

How many more expository sermons did he have in him? Were his teachings planting seeds of thought for future use? Were the community outreaches he'd gotten the church involved in actually helping stop the tide of regression society seemed to face?

He'd actually raised the possibility of retirement with his wife, Alice, that morning. He was becoming increasingly conscious that the number of messages left to deliver was finite, and that Father Time, with the intent of offering Rev.

Hasbro his own private garden tomb, was reaching out to him. A wave of melancholy swept over Bill Hasbro the Notre Dame grad who'd chosen the ministry to transform lives only to discover his had been the first to change.

"Oh, silly, silly man. Never fear, for can't you see he's not here? And if he isn't here, what could you have possibly to fear?

*Don't you realize, you're looking at **hope**? Understand why you followed your calling. It was hope. Hope to shake the world by its foundation into a better place. Do you remember the quiver in your voice as you stood to deliver your first sermon? Do you not recall how your knees went numb as your legs locked up while sharing the first message of so many to come?*

Hope kept you going. A hope that is only present in a future laying on the horizon that is waiting to be seized. A future where the end is beyond sight.

Now, you see the end and you doubt the hope. You question the change. The person who was here is gone but the hope isn't. The absence of his body means the hope is alive and thriving in the people you serve.

Take heart. Finish your task. More of those people still need to discover hope. One day you'll be reunited with the source of your hope.

"Bill. Bill!"

"Huh?" A shiver went up Rev. Hasbro's spine.

"Are you ok, Bill?" Cole asked out of concern.

"Oh, yes. Just a chill in here, I guess."

"You seemed like you were zoned out there for a second. You turned pale. Are you sure you're, ok?" Cole reiterated

Rev. Hasbro smiled, "Better than you can imagine."

Stepping back out into the sunshine, Rev. Hasbro looked up, feeling the best he had in ages. In fact, if he could've gotten away with it, he would've broken out into a sermon right there on the spot.

.   .   .   .

Monique had found a shady place to sit. The grounds of the Garden Tomb were everything that the Garden of Gethsemane was not. The floral assortment was outstanding and well groomed.

The layout of the grounds encouraged visitors to enter a respective, sacred, mode. The paths led through peaceful settings where benches were positioned to encourage visitors to take a moment and become one with the environment surrounding them.

Monique noticed there were quite a few people sitting and reading scriptures. One person she passed seemed to be writing poetry while another had been praying.

Her feet aching, Monique claimed a spot of her own. She saw Rev. Hasbro exit the tomb. He looked so content. "I bet he never worries about anything," she thought.

"There is hope," a voice whispered from behind. Monique jerked around but there wasn't anyone present. Then she glanced around to see if anyone had noticed her strange behavior but apparently it'd gone undetected.

"Hope," she whispered to herself.

"Are you ready?"

"What? For hope?" Monique answered.

"What are you talking about?" Cole asked.

Monique jerked her head up, "Sorry, I was lost in thought there for a second."

"You know, I'm beginning to think that everyone has been out in the sun a bit too long. I just thought you might like to browse the gift shop on the way out."

Monique smiled, "Sure, let's see what you can buy me."

CHAPTER 10: Tourists & Migrants Pt. 2

"How many more gifts are on the list?" Cole asked Monique.

Monique replied, "Well, we've already picked up Eric something in Jerusalem. And we bought Randy and your parent's gifts at the Dead Sea, remember?"

"I still think that vendor was gauging us. Who does that leave then?" Cole wondered.

"Really, all we need is to find something for Mulu. After all, she's watching Eric for a two long weeks."

Cole grinned, "Sanity isn't something you buy in a place like this."

"We have to get her something even if it's only a T-shirt or trinket." Monique stated. Cole let out a grunt as he was elbowed from behind by a passing shopper.

The Carmiel Market at the intersection of Allenby St. and Hamelech George in the heart of Tel Aviv was its usual shoulder to shoulder, move in mass, busy self. The open air market, sealed off for pedestrians only, was the main gathering point for bargain hunters and not for the timid.

"Oh, we can't forget Aunt Patty, your Uncle Charlie and especially my sister Helene. She'd kill me if I didn't pick up some kind of souvenir for her."

"Ok, that's enough. Every time I ask, the list grows. Forget everyone except Mulu and your sister," Cole suggested.

"What about the others?"

"Do you really want to be out here all day?" Cole asked.

Monique looked around, "Not really."

"Why did they bring us here, anyway? We shopped in the Old City. Isn't one open, chaotic, frenzied free-for-all bazaar enough?" Cole was fed up with the afternoon's tour schedule.

"I know, I know," Monique agreed.

"Why, didn't they just take us to a mall if all they wanted us to do was shop?" Cole quipped.

"You? You would go to a mall?" Monique's shocked expression caught the attention of the man selling the wares on the other side of the booth where they were standing.

Cole glanced around, "Compared to this? Gladly."

"Wow, there's a first. Mr. Cole Tarkington wants to shop at a mall," Monique broke out in laughter which enticed an aggravated glare from Cole.

"Look, dear, let us find a T-shirt or something for Mulu. I will hunt for Helene later. What do you say we get the T-shirt, escape from the tour group, and do some of that *us* time back at the hotel that we agreed would be our real mission on this trip?" Monique suggested with a grin.

"Now you're talking. Deal." Cole's spirit suddenly lightened up.

"What are you two tour birds talking about?" Sis. Gladys asked with an armful of goods which Cole caught as they started sliding out of her arms.

"Thank you, Cole. Isn't this place great?" Sis. Gladys exclaimed.

Monique shook her head in mockingly agreement, "Oh, absolutely."

"Cole, you're a man. Can you come over here and see if you think my son Johnny would like this belt buckle?" Sis. Gladys was started to head toward a different shop.

"Go!" Cole urged Monique. "Go, do that thing and I'll meet you right back here."

"Ok," Monique said.

Cole mouthed the word, "Hurry."

Monique hustled off in the opposite direction. She knew Helene wouldn't really appreciate any of the cheap merchandise being passed off in this bazaar. Most of the stuff was knock off designer wares, T-shirts for tourists, and little artsy items that local artists probably couldn't get buyers for anywhere else.

Still, Monique figured Mulu would settle for a T-shirt or two from Israel. After all, t-shirts were mandatory college dress code and you couldn't own too many of them.

What kind of T-shirt was the question at hand. There were plenty implying Israel's military might in a joking fashion but Monique wanted to get Mulu something leaning a little less to the violent side. Everything else she picked up to examine seemed to exhibit a print that was big and gaudy.

A sigh escaped Monique as she leaned her head to one side to take a deep breath. Then she straightened up, having detected a figure she hadn't expected. Circling another merchant a short distance away was the lady she'd encountered at Caesarea. She was cradling the baby in her arms.

"That tattoo stands out even in a crowd like this," Monique thought.

Monique desired to duck out of sight but in this open area there was nowhere to hide. That instinct was followed by an impulse to traipse over and re-introduce herself. She actually took the first step in that direction but stopped because the lady was talking to a hardened-looking character.

The conspicuous person's thinning hair was brushed to one side. Even from this distance, Monique distinguished that his nose had been broken more than once and though he was overweight, his arms hung by his side like a boxer waiting for a scrap. The aged lines on his face were frozen in place from an inner coldness.

Was that the baby's father? Monique considered it might be since the conversation seemed pretty intense.

"What you doing bringing a baby down here?" Yuri was perturbed with Lady Marina.

"What else am I suppose to do with her?" Lady Marina snapped.

"I don't know. I don't care. This is no place for children of any age," Yuri scolded.

"Why not? What looks more natural than me shopping with a baby?" Lady Marina shot back.

"What do you mean, 'natural'? This … this …" Yuri motioned with his arms at the baby, "this is not natural. And in your case, it can be classified as plain abnormal."

"What are you talking about? I'd be a good mother if I chose to be," Lady Marina insisted.

Yuri huffed, "Where did you get it?"

"Does it really matter?" Lady Marina retorted.

Yuri pointed at the baby, "This is no monkey."

Lady Marina squirmed at the thought that Yuri knew so many intimate details of her personal life. Furthermore, she knew he wouldn't flinch in plying that information to his advantage.

"That's right. I know about that pet you kept around your office back in Addis Ababa. This baby, you're holding, requires more than a banana." Yuri's bite had venom to it.

"I know. I'll handle it. But I can't just abandon Katrina," Lady Marina argued.

Yuri was incredulous, "You named her?"

"Well, yes! A baby has to have a name, you know. You can't very well just go around calling the baby 'it' all the time. What kind of man are you?"

Yuri grabbed Lady Marina's arm forcing her to tighten her grasp on Katrina. "The kind of man who looks after his own interests. The kind of man who'll take whatever steps are necessary to ensure that his business isn't jeopardized by the infatuations of underlings."

Yuri relaxed his grip.

"I've always thought highly of you, Lady Marina. You're tougher than most guys I have on the payroll. You put business first and until now, you've been loyal to the job. After all you've been through, I'd hate to see throw that reputation aside and risk everything you've gained so far."

172

"Tell me, Yuri, is being all that enough?" Lady Marina asked.

A tone of sadness crept into Yuri's voice, "Oh, my poor, dear. Don't you understand? What are your chances of survival if it isn't?"

Lady Marina gazed down at Katrina who was sleeping in spite of all the surrounding noise.

"Look, Lady Marina, I need to know I can count on you. I need to be assured you're focused on your work. If I can't be confident of that fact, well, let's just say other arrangements will have to be made. You get my drift?" Yuri asked.

Lady Marina paused before answering, "You can count on me. You always have in the past and you can in the future."

Yuri shifted from his confrontational stance to present a softer tone, "Guy says you had a problem with the other night."

The image of the women chained up in the warehouse like animals headed to market had understandably been ingrained into Lady Marina's memory. "Me? Nah."

"It isn't pretty. I'll grant you that. And you being a woman, I can see where these situations might be, shall we say more delicate. But it is what it is. Business is business. Don't forget that. There is a high demand in that market and with high demand comes high profits," Yuri said as though explaining a company's bottom line to a union representative.

Yuri looked over Lady Marina's shoulder. In the mass of people, he spotted a lady seemingly lurking at a T-shirt stand. Instead of flipping through designs though, she was intently curious about their conversation.

He reached down on the table behind him to retrieve a compact mirror. Flipping it open, he held it up in front of Lady Marina asking, "See anything that interests you?"

Lady Marina clutched the baby a little tighter as she spotted Monique standing in the distance. "I bumped into that lady up at Caesarea. I'd never seen her before then."

"Police?" Yuri asked.

"I don't think so but I can't say for certain. Maybe, its only coincidence," Marina suggested.

"Coincidence," Yuri huffed, again.

"Follow me," he ordered.

The pair mingled into the crowd of shoppers, moving at a snail pace through the market. Heading toward the Carmiel bus station, the market turned from clothes and knick knacks to food staples. Yuri stopped long enough to snatch an apple and sneak a glance behind them to making sure Monique was still in tow.

At a juncture in the path, Yuri made eye contact with a young man propped up on a bicycle. Discreetly, Yuri reached down to his cellphone, and as quickly as any teenage girl could've done with her friends when spotting a group of boys, he texted a message.

Within seconds, the boy on the bike heard the alert system ring on his phone. Looking down, the kid scanned the message before slipping the phone into his pocket and setting the bike into action. Yuri and Lady Marina moved passed the kid, shuffling around to appear like any other couple out shopping. The boy, half-a-peddle at a time, made his way through the masses who anxiously tried side-stepping him while swearing at his audacity to ride in such a crowded place.

By this time, Monique had been distracted by a tap on the shoulder.

"Can you tell me what you think of this?" Elain asked in Hebrew as she held up a blouse.

"Sorry, I don't speak Hebrew." Monique's reply only prompted Elain to repeat the question in English.

"Is it for you?" Monique asked, trying to size it up in a hurry.

"Of course," Elain stated with a smile.

There wasn't time to compare fashion points as a cry rose from the crowd. Monique spun around in time to see the boy on the bike rolling directly in her at her. She had only a split-second to step out of his way. Still, the handle bar caught her, sending her backward into a table full of wares which toppled over and smacked her head.

Elain, eyeing the blouse, wasn't afforded the split-second Monique and was totally blindsided by the biker. The force sent her sprawling forward, knocking her out as she hit the ground.

A crowd of people swarmed down on Monique. For Monique, whose head was ringing and her eyes were out of focus, the mass of hands reaching out to touch her made her feel like part of the merchandise.

The shopkeeper was livid, letting the kid on the bike feel his wrath and the crowd was just as enraged. For his part, the bike rider apologized profusely but it carried no weight with one older lady who swung her shopping bag into his back side.

Monique was lifted up by sturdy hands and someone in the confusion managed to carry out a chair for her to sit on as they removed her from the main thoroughfare.

"Ok, maybe, Mulu's gift can wait," she thought as she watched the efforts to revive Elain.

.   .   .   .

Two uniformed policemen, speaking Hebrew in their radios, were practically pushing people aside as they jogged past Cole.

"I wonder what is going on?" Cole asked aloud.

"In this crowd? Probably a shoplifter," Rev. Hasbro stated.

Cole chuckled though still scanning the crowd, hoping to spot a familiar piece of clothing that might give away Monique's position.

Rev. Hasbro asked, "Who you looking for?"

"Mo," Cole answered.

"Is she shopping?"

"She's trying to find something for Mulu and maybe her sister. What about you? You have gifts to buy?" Cole asked.

Rev. Hasbro smiled, "I bought Alice something in Jerusalem. I'm not worrying about anyone else."

"It's too bad she couldn't come," Cole noted.

"I can't get that woman to leave St. Clair except once a year to visit a cousin in Pittsburgh. Besides, if she was here, I'd be shopping all day," Rev. Hasbro joked.

177

"Is there something that you need to buy?" Rev. Hasbro asked.

"No," Cole answered with frustrated impatience.

"Want to escape?" Rev. Hasbro asked.

"What about the rest of the tour group?" Cole wondered as he looked behind him at Sis. Gladys who had become preoccupied with haggling over a necklace; should she pay the equivalent of seven dollars or only five?

Rev. Hasbro motioned for Cole to follow. "They're scattered all over this market. Come on."

"But Mo …"

"She'll find us," Rev. Hasbro assured him.

"But we were going …"and then Cole reminded himself who he was speaking too.

"Never mind," he said and followed Rev. Hasbro up toward Allenby Street where they exited the market, celebrating in being able to gain a measure of breathing space.

Where they paused at though proved to be as entertaining as any merchant they had seen all day. There on the ground, positioned between the market and the street, was a Jesus wannabe.

The man was cloaked in a white robe and sported a beard about the same length as Cole remembered seeing on a picture of Jesus hanging in the church vestibule as a kid. Bread rolls were stacked on the dirty yellow blanket where he was sitting as though the food represented an offering.

The Jesus wannabe had his legs crossed as though he was a guru waiting for the meaning of life to reveal itself. A portrait of himself was leaning up against an empty jar which invited donations from passer-bys.

Sitting on the blanket with him were two followers. There was a girl whose dirty hair at some point had been a beautiful brunette. Her jeans were ragged and from the holes in her shirt, Cole guessed she'd been on the street for a while.

The other 'disciple' was a guitar strumming lad whose soles on his tennis shoes were splitting apart. From the way he looked at the girl, Cole concluded the spiritual and lust were pretty crowded in sharing the same heart.

"This I have to see," Rev. Hasbro said, leading them up to the blanket.

The self-appointed messiah tried to appear so focused that he couldn't be bothered by the curious stranger.

"So you're the Messiah?" Rev. Hasbro winked at Cole.

"True believers know this to be the case," the man declared in an accent reminiscent of Seattle rather than Tel Aviv.

"Well, if this is the extent of your followers, there may be hope for humanity after all," Rev. Hasbro came off more condescending than he intended.

"I am here to show the way of enlightenment," the man announced.

"I'm not sure I want to be enlightened by a guy who can't find the shower," Cole rebutted.

"Does it bother you that people don't believe in you?" Rev. Hasbro asked.

"I am above answering to others," the man scooted into a more comfortable position on the blanket.

"At this point, I am sure you are," Rev. Hasbro replied with a grin.

"Besides, a prophet is not honored in his own country."

"From your accent, I'd say your own country is back in the States. So, basically, you're just being rejected worldwide." Cole's statement caused the guitar player to quite strumming. The girl moved closer to her leader who put his arm on hers for comfort.

"So you've read the Bible?" Rev. Hasbro asked.

"I have," the man affirmed.

"Maybe you should think hard about taking it to heart before it's too late," Rev. Hasbro suggested before turning away with Cole.

Leaving the market messiah behind, the pair pointed themselves in the direction of the sea and made their break.

"For an ancient land, there are a lot of modern people here," Rev. Hasbro noted. With the mix of people they found themselves among, they could just have easily been in Chicago.

Cole halted.

"What is it?" Rev. Hasbro asked.

Cole pointed across the street to a sign that was the last thing he expected to find on this tour. In big green and yellow colors with a lion in the middle, were the words, "Little Addis Ababa – Ethiopian Food."

"Look, Bill, have you ever had any Ethiopian food?" Cole asked.

"No, can't say I have," Rev. Hasbro answered.

"Well, you can't find any back in St. Clair that is for sure."

Rev. Hasbro agreed, "Yeah, I suppose you wouldn't be able too."

"Well, now that I see that sign, I have a hankering for some. What do you say?"

"Beats shopping back at the market." Rev. Hasbro consented.

The two found the nearest crosswalk and headed for the restaurant whose door was propped open.

CHAPTER ELEVEN: The Date

"Dr. Peer, please, report to the nurse's station," the page over the hospital intercom requested.

Dr. Yossi Peer stood in front of the elevator watching the floors tick off one light at a time when he heard the announcement. The elevator sounded a familiar *ding* as he looked at his watch before double-timing it back to the nurse's station.

"What is it Megi?" he asked.

"Dr. Zarouk requests your presence in room 302." The turned up expression Megi gave, spoke as much to her low esteem of Dr. Zarouk as the clash of personalities she knew existed between the two doctors.

"But I'm off duty now," Yossi complained.

"Date?"

"Not everyone rejects me," Yossi replied.

"It wasn't a rejection," Megi playfully stated.

"When someone goes '*no, no, no*' that pretty much comes across as a rejection to me," Yossi told her.

"Ok, so technically it was," Megi admitted.

"Technically? Wow, feel the emotion."

"I told you, you aren't Jewish so I can't date you," Megi shot back.

"You could try it just once?" Yossi teased knowing very well that his interest had been casual to start with and that Megi wasn't about to bend her beliefs to become another number in his contact list.

"Dr. Zarouk insisted," Megi reminded him.

"Thanks, Megi." Yossi resigned himself to leaving the friendly barbs for the slicing tit-for-tat of Dr. Zarouk awaiting him in room 302.

"Ah, there you are, Dr. Peer. You've been keeping me waiting," Dr. Ali Zarouk scolded.

"Sorry, I answered the page as quickly as … Elain?" Yossi was surprised to find Elain sitting on an examination table. She offered up a weak wave.

"This woman says she is a patient of yours, is that true?" Dr. Zarouk asked.

Yossi readily answered, "Yes."

"Then I thought you might want to take a quick glance at these x-rays." Dr. Zarouk handed over the film.

"What happened?" Yossi inquired, still a little shocked.

"There was a pedestrian accident down at the Carmiel Market. She got knocked out cold," Dr. Zarouk explained.

"In short, a bicycle ran me over," Elain said.

"A bicycle?" Yossi reviewed the pictures of Elain's head.

"It's more common than people think," Dr. Zarouk commented.

"These look fine," Yossi declared.

"She didn't take my word for it," Dr. Zarouk said with stinging resentment in his voice.

"I preferred hearing it from someone I knew," Elain admitted.

The door to the room opened and in walked Adi. The couple quickly hugged while Elain assured him that she was fine.

"How is it this woman is a patient of yours? I screen the patients assigned to you and I don't recall her." Yossi sensed Dr. Zarouk's temperature starting to boil.

"You wouldn't. I go to Church with them and they asked if I would advise them on some insemination options," Yossi responded.

"Insemination? I don't approve patients for that," Dr. Zarouk angrily declared.

"There's no hospital policy against it," Yossi countered.

Dr. Zarouk reiterated, "But, I don't approve patients for those procedures."

"Why not?" Yossi was perplexed by Dr. Zarouk's groundless arbitration in the matter.

"If they can't have children, then it must be Allah's will for this to be so," Dr. Zarouk definitively stated leaving Yossi stunned by a fellow practitioner taking such a medieval stance.

"Surely, you don't believe that?"

"This woman has no right, defying Allah's will," Dr. Zarouk angrily repeated.

"My wife is sitting right here," Adi reminded Dr. Zarouk.

Elain stood. Adi held on to her in case she felt woozy from the injury. "Thanks honey but I can handle this. First off, I don't worry about *Allah* or any religions that allows the likes of you to dictate to women what they can and cannot do."

Adi couldn't let his wife be the only one standing up against such nonsense. "If this isn't hospital policy, then maybe I should talk to the hospital administrator about your conduct."

"Well that won't be necessary," Dr. Zarouk insisted.

"I'll be the one to decide that," Adi retorted.

"I would advise against it. Any complaint against me would only result in your wife's condition being made public. I'm sure you're not interested in having that happen, are you?"

Adi glanced at Yossi for confirmation.

"I'm afraid Dr. Zarouk is correct." Yossi reluctantly admitted.

"See!" Dr. Zarouk gloated.

"It's because you're an Arab isn't it?" Adi angrily said.

"I can assure you my race has nothing to do in how I do my job," Dr. Zarouk shot back before Yossi stepped between the pair to keep the argument from escalating.

"Adi, why don't you take Elain out into the hallway and I'll join you in a minute." Adi and Elain followed Yossi's suggestion and left the room but not before Adi flashed a devastating glare at Dr. Zarouk.

"What is wrong with you?" Yossi demanded.

"Nothing! But rest assure I am going to file a report about this to the administrator's office. You cannot undermine my authority this way."

"What? Because I see them on an issue you don't like?" Yossi sarcastically said.

"This isn't America."

"I'm well aware of that," Yossi scoffed.

"I am your supervisor. You cannot go behind my back," Dr. Zarouk insisted.

"Instead of a supervisor, maybe you should worry about being a doctor to everyone first. If you want to report me, fine! Report me, I don't care," Yossi told him.

"Really? Because I've seen your file and frankly, another page in it might finish you as a doctor all together," Dr. Zarouk threatened.

"Well, we'll see, won't we?" Yossi stormed out of the room.

.   .   .   .

"You're late," Desica greeted Yossi in a tone not impressed by his tardiness.

"So I am." He noticed Desica had dressed up for the occasion with a summer-like blue dress that included a strip of lace around the shoulders. The gold necklace with an emerald as its apex complimented both her eyes and the dress.

"And you brought someone to our date," Desica said with a mocking-pleasantry that alerted Yossi to the fact the date was off to a rocky start.

"So did you," Yossi retorted noticing Lihi.

"I just thought I'd say hello but maybe I should wait outside." Lihi started rising from her seat.

Yossi held up his hand, stopping her. "No, it's ok."

"Good. I'm really just waiting on Naftali anyway," Lihi explained.

Yossi smiled. "Let me guess, he's late."

"Always," Lihi and Desica confirmed in unison.

Turning toward his guest, Yossi introduced them, "This is Elain and Adi. It's a long story but they were patients at the hospital, and I know them from church, and well, they needed relief from the day," Yossi explained.

"Nothing serious, I hope?" Desica said.

"Bump on the head. I got smacked down by a bicycle in the Carmiel Market," Elain replied.

"That place is treacherous. You really have to stay on your toes there," Lihi said.

Desica shrugged off the unanticipated. " Well, the more the merrier."

CHAPTER 12: Tourists & Immigrants Pt. 2

The inside of the Ethiopian restaurant was shaded from
the baking atmosphere outside by its lack of windows.
Even though the door was often left open by customers
who assumed it'd shut properly on its own, the sun had no
way to bore it's wilting powers onto diners as the air
conditioner kept a steady breeze of relief blowing.

If you'd never been to Ethiopia before, 'Little Addis
Ababa' was intent to convey a taste of the place. In the end
the proprietor Abby, a mother of three who as an olim had
been in the country 25 years, wanted to satiate the palate
and placate the culturally curious with an atmospheric
presentation that watered the simple seeds of imagination.

The brown walls were of a black and green stripe design.
Several pieces of Ethiopian art hung on the walls depicting
the lives of the olim who'd created them. Overall, the place
was clean and fresh, especially for a restaurant situated off
a busy thoroughfare where the air churned the dusty runoff
of traffic.

Music that was a combination of Israeli folk meets house,
blared over a sound system meshing the modern world with
ancient roots.

The aroma trickling past the noses, originated from a ceaseless supply of incense strategically positioned around the restaurant. The smell drummed up the sensations of ancient woods, exotic spices or the recollection of an iconic monastery on a remote mountain. The atmosphere along with a menu consisting of njera and wut brought the streets of Addis Ababa as close to Tel Aviv as possible without making a trip to Ben Gurion airport.

As Cole Tarkington and Bill Hasbro entered the restaurant, Cole took a big whiff. The smells triggered a sudden longing to return to villages he'd once visited. A smile broke out as though a door in the back room of the mind had been unlocked.

The men took a seat as their eyes adjusted to the comparative shade inside. It was then that Cole noticed a familiar face staring at him from a nearby table. It took a moment for recognition to set in.

"Yossi?"

"Cole?" Yossi replied equally astonished.

Cole gleefully shook Yossi's hand. "What are you doing here?"

"I can ask the same thing," Yossi replied.

"This is the most crowded date I've ever been on," Desica observed with a smile.

191

"Hope we're not intruding," Cole said.

"Not at all," Desica quipped.

"Abby, we'll need a couple more menus," Yossi shouted out before managing the introductions as Cole and Rev. Hasbro took up seats at the table. What had been planned as a romantic, impressionable date for two became a joyous feast for seven.

.   .   .   .

The bicycle with the chipping blue paint and a rusty chain darted down the sidewalk past a park, on a piece of ground situated between the New Central Bus Station and the old one, in the Neve Sha'anan District of Tel Aviv. The neighborhood was populated by lounging immigrants from various nations but mostly from Africa.

Even though the sun hadn't set yet on the day, many in the park, jobless and clinging to the bottom rung of Israeli society, were already buzzed from the bottles they were passing around. Drinking and swapping stories of lands with others suffering the same fate was as good as way as any to pass the time.

As Peter Israel peddled past the Old Central bus station, he glanced down at his watch, its two coordinated hand confirming that He was running late. The Ethiopian Jewish son named after an American aid worker who saved his family during a drought, Peter was increasingly distraught over fate's infringement on every little aspect of his life. His life was spiraling out of control to the point he couldn't even arrive at work on time.

"You're late," Abby barked without bothering to check the time as Peter entered the restaurant's back entrance into the restaurant's kitchen.

"I know. I am sorry," Peter apologized parking his bike inside the door.

"It's the third time this week," Abby warned.

"I know, I know," Peter replied.

"I know you know, but how do you expect me to run a business like this?" Abby shouted.

"What do you want me to say?" Peter asked exasperated.

"That you'll be on time. This is what I want you to say," Abby told him.

"But Sofia ..."

"Your wife belongs in a hospital," Abby blurted out.

"She won't go! The doctors say there is nothing they can do and so she refuses to go," Peter explained.

"Well, you're going to have to do something or at least get someone to help you out," Abby said.

Abby wasn't without sympathy. Peter had worked for her for three years and had been valuable, even unwavering, in his work ethic. But as Sofia's condition gradually worsened, Abby had witnessed Peter's transformation into only a shell of his former self. While that change may have been natural under his circumstances, Abby was torn between her friendship with Peter and her role as entrepreneur whose business relied on dependability.

"I've tried," Peter insisted.

"Ok, ok," Abby said as she stacked a tray full of soft drinks.

"There's a group of seven out there. Take these drinks to them then come back and start on the dishes," Abby instructed.

"Yes ma'am." Peter swooped up the tray and headed through the swinging door into the main dining area.

It wasn't until he arrived at the table of chattering customers that Peter got a good glance of whom he was serving. With the first drink in one hand, and the tray being balanced by the other, Peter's eyes widened, he straightened up as a tremor ran through his body.

Talk in the group simmered down as the waiter made his odd appearance. The waiter was acting like he was in shock, prompting Yossi to ask, "Are you ok?"

The waiter stammered. Everyone else hung in anticipation of the words trying to cross his lips. Suddenly, in his excitement, the waiter lost control of the tray, which shifted on his arm and began to slide toward the guests.

Peter's instinct was to catch the tray but as he moved to do that, with his other hand, he dumped the first drink on Cole. A millisecond later, the drinks on the tray tumbled onto Yossi, Desica and Lihi. Rev. Hasbro caught the brunt of one full glass all by himself. Adi and Elain being at the other end managed to miss the tidal wave of caffeinated sugar.

A look of *this can't be happening to me* bewilderment crossed the group's faces. For Peter, the reaction was one of genuine horror not only that he'd committed such a faux pas but had done so with this particular group.

"Not the kind of hospitality I was expecting," Rev. Hasbro commented as he took a razor thin napkin from Adi that proved useless in wiping up the mess.

"Yeah, I know what you mean," Cole said.

"Your dress," Yossi noted to Desica.

"This old thing? Don't worry about it." Desica was kicking herself for having spent so much time getting ready for this date.

"Mr. Cole, I am so sorry!!!!" Peter exclaimed.

"Mr. Yossi, let me get that for you," Finding a towel, Peter quickly began drying off the table and the bottom of Yossi's pants.

"What have you done?" Abby screamed as she came out to survey the scene.

"I accidently spilled the drinks on Mr. Cole and Mr. Yossi and guests," Peter confessed while still trying to dry up the mess up, but the towel was now soaked and sticky, making matters much worse.

There it was again. Cole and Yossi glanced at each other hoping the other could decipher what was running through their mind.

"Your dinner will be on the establishment." Abby restrained both her embarrassment and anger.

Turning to Peter, she said, "You clean this up and then I want to see you in the back."

"Wait!" Cole said.

Yossi stopped Peter. "What's your name?"

"Peter, sir."

Cole chimed in, "What we're getting at is that you know our names, I mean you said them twice now but we don't know yours which means …"

"We've never met," Yossi finished.

"Well, this will be an introduction you won't forget," Desica noted while Lihi snapped a photo on her camera and emailed it to Naftali whom she was still waiting on to show.

"Maybe he knows you, Yossi. You come in here a lot?" Elain suggested.

"No that's not it," Yossi replied.

"How do you know us?" Cole demanded.

"Answer the gentlemen," Abby ordered.

"From Ethiopia. I was visiting a cousin who married this tribal leader's daughter. We made the journey to the wedding. See, she belonged to the Horro tribe. I was with the Horro the day you came there."

Cole and Yossi leaned back in their chairs. Now, the situation was making sense.

"Who are the Horro?" Lihi asked.

"You two? You are the missionaries who did the wonders among the Horro?" Abby hurriedly grabbed clean towels to help Peter finish cleaning up the mess even handing one to Rev. Hasbro whose pants were ruined by the spill.

"I saw them with my own two eyes. They were with the Teguash," Peter told Abby.

Cole couldn't be sure, but it sounded like Abby was praying under her breath and the harder she prayed, the harder she wiped.

"You did wondrous things there. Many miracles," Peter said.

"Is he talking about Ethiopia?" Rev. Hasbro asked. Cole gave him an affirmative nod of the head.

"Did you two walk on water or something?" Desica asked.

"Not hardly, although our getting out of there alive was no less a miracle. Cole here was stabbed and nearly died on us," Yossi told her.

"Seriously?" Desica exclaimed.

"I am Jewish but I see the many feats you did. The story of the Teguash is legend and you were part of it," Peter boasted.

Peter stopped as though a vision was appearing before his eyes. "You are an answer to prayer."

"I am sure prayer had a lot to do with us going to the Horro." Cole dismissed the praise being showered on him and Yossi as overrated hype.

"No, no. I mean, you are an answer to prayer now," Peter insisted.

"How is that?" Yossi asked.

"My wife, Sofia, is very ill. You must come. You have the power to heal her," Peter stated.

Cole stopped him. "Whoa. We don't heal. God does."

"But he works through you. Please, come see my Sofia," Peter begged.

"Well, maybe later…" Rev. Hasbro started to suggest.

"No, it must be now. She is so ill," Peter explained.

"I don't know. I mean, we need to get back to the tour group," Cole stated.

Peter pleaded, "Her life depends on you."

Abby backed Peter up, "She is very ill. Your presence could make a difference."

Cole had an uneasy feeling about the whole situation. On the other hand, he wasn't a fan of coincidence either. What if the whole afternoon's events had been leading to this moment?

Cole looked at Yossi, "What do you think?"

Yossi shrugged.

"Maybe you should go," Desica suggested.

"What could it hurt? Besides, God has worked in stranger ways," Rev. Hasbro pointed out.

"You guys might be right." Cole conceded.

Cole looked at Yossi who was sharing the same doubts as he was. After a moment, the verdict was clear.

Abby insisted the dinner was on the house. Yossi left enough money with Desica, who figured this was a first date worthy of a blog posting when she got home, to make sure that Adi and Elain were able to catch a taxi. Lihi received a text from Naftali saying he was only ten minutes away which meant she would be leaving shortly as well.

That left Cole, Yossi, and Rev. Hasbro who despite being stained from a cascade of soft drinks, descended into a cab of their own with Peter and headed toward the Neve Sha'anan part of town.

.　　.　　.　　.　　.　　.　　.

Cole didn't know the age of the building where Peter lived but it certainly showed wear beyond its years. Cracks in every window pane on the first floor gave a warning of the despair to be found inside. The bashed-in entryway forebode of neglect both of the residence and the residents dwelling there.

Trash and food remnants lay outside doorways. As they climbed the stairs, a female passing them in shorts and a tank paused long enough to make a provocative suggestion only to be chased away by Peter.

"My daughter is at a friend's across the street," Peter explained while reaching for his key.

"How old is she?" Cole asked.

"Two," Peter replied.

The stench inside Peter's flat on the fourth floor of the building stifled the senses with the inhalation of decay. The flat itself consisted of a main room that was both bedroom and living room.

Sofia lay stretched out on a mattress thrown flat on the floor. The mattress had been overused. Without sheets to cover it up, many stains, evidence of Sofia's illness, blotched the mattress which also had big rips exposing the stuffing.

A filthy sheet covered Sofia who never acknowledged the group's arrival. As though a statuette in a dark garden, her head never moved off the pillow where it rested.

There was a small fresh puddle of blood mixed with vomit that had run down the side of the mattress. Sofia hadn't been able to get her head over the side of the mattress at the proper moment.

Peter grabbed a nearby towel, and began clearing up the small puddle.

"Look, who is here!" Peter whispered to Sofia without receiving a response.

Yossi bent down to check her pulse. It was so weak that he bent over to hear her heart. The beat was too faint to get a bead on it. The signs of lesions, and the frailness of Sofia's body, indicated to Yossi why what she was suffering.

Cole knew by Yossi's expression that the prognostic outcome was not what Peter was wishing.

"Does she have AIDS?" Yossi asked.

Rev. Hasbro reacted to the question by taking a step backward.

"Yes," Peter said.

"Have you been tested?" Yossi asked.

"I am afraid so. She didn't know when we - I mean we were husband and wife," Peter answered.

"How'd she get it?" As soon as Cole voiced the question he knew how stupid he was sounding.

"It's my fault. I couldn't support a family with that waiter's job." Peter sounded angry at himself.

Cole turned to Rev. Hasbro who simply said, "Maybe we should say a prayer."

"Yes, pray. Please, pray. Make her well," Peter begged.

Leaning down, Peter whispered in his wife's ear, "These are the men who were with the Teguash. They are going to heal you."

"We didn't say that," Yossi cautioned.

"You have healed others why not her?" Peter clamored.

Rev. Hasbro interjected, "It isn't in our hands, young man."

"You've done it before. You can do it again," Peter yelled.

Distraught, Peter leaned across and grabbed Yossi by the shirt. "You have to try. What good is your faith, what good is your God if not for something like this?"

Yossi slowly loosened Peter's grip and glanced over at Cole and Rev. Hasbro.

Cole didn't know how the others felt but inside, he was hesitant. While he didn't know Peter personally, it seemed to Cole that nothing good was to come out of whatever they did here. The last thing he wanted to do was lead Peter on.

"What do you say?" Rev. Hasbro asked Cole.

The Third Sister had seen this scene many times in many lands. The scenario had played itself out throughout the pages of human history. She had even experienced the pain of illness and loss herself.

Wounds of the heart are not easily closed. The memory is never erased and the feeling of throwing yourself at the base of the savior's cross in vain choked the very tears it produced.

Looking on, the Third Sister had seen the end result. The remedy was clear in her timeless vision.

"All the ingredients are here," was the subtle whisper in Cole's ear.

Cole was afraid to react to what he was hearing least the others denigrate him for it.

*"There is faith. There is hope. But most importantly, there is **love**," the voice continued.*

"Can you not grant your neighbor a request in his hour of need? Can you not bring your love to bear to ease his mind? Is your belief so rigid that you'd put your image above his sorrow?" the voice questioned.

Cole thought for a second. Was he really more worried about how he'd look at the end of this than trying to help?

*"Act out of **love**," the voice commanded.*

"Cole?" Rev. Hasbro said.

"Hmmm?"

"What do you think?" Rev. Hasbro asked again.

"I think we should pray," Cole said bringing a smile from Peter who made way for the group to surround Sofia.

Praying for someone you don't know can be problematic. One wishes to avoid making false assumptions about the person, misstating elements in their life, or in the case of Sofia, indicating how God may answer such a serious issue.

Rev. Hasbro led the group in prayer. He asked for healing. He asked for God's will to be done. He asked for a miracle. Cole and Yossi joined in while Peter held Sofia' hand waiting for a miracle to be sent down from the divine.

As the prayer for Sofia wound down, Rev. Hasbro felt a need to pray for Peter as well so he changed the focus of what he was saying to do just that.

It was at this moment that Peter felt an explosion of grief followed by a rush of love. For it was during a prayer whose words became blocked out that he realized his wish would not be granted. A wish he'd held onto for months.

That realization made him aware of how much he loved Sofia. The good times, the hard times, the memories he privately cherished, even the fights over what now seemed trivial matters, had occurred because of their love for each other.

Yossi hadn't gotten so involved with the prayer to forget about Sofia. He'd kept peeking at her laying there helpless. How many people had he seen in this situation during his career? People trying to do what they need to do to survive only to be taken down by a scourge of nature.

Without warning, Sofia let out an audible exhale. Her head flipped to one side and stream of dribble flowed from the corner of her mouth.

Everyone in the room looked at her with their own level of expectations. Rev. Hasbro was the only one who bothered to keep praying although his intensity tapered off.

"Did you see that?" Peter said, although somewhere inside he sensed his hope might be manufactured.

"Yeah," Cole could tell by Yossi's tone that he wasn't as optimistic.

Yossi checked the pulse in a couple places then looked up and simply said, "I'm sorry, Peter."

"What?"

Rev. Hasbro tried putting his hand on Peter's shoulder but the man moved away, not wanting to be touched.

"You were with the Teguash," Peter muttered in shock.

Cole spoke up, "I told you that we couldn't make any promises."

"But I have seen what you can do with my own eyes. My own eyes!"

"The decision isn't ours," Cole stated.

"My Sofia." Peter began weeping as he dropped to his knees to hug his wife's corpse.

Cole bent down to look at Peter directly.

"How will I live without her? She's gone," Peter stammered through the tears.

"But she went with love. You gave her the most important thing you could, love. The way you cared for her, only someone who truly loved her would've done that. Asking us to come here to pray, again a sign of love. Don't you think she knew that? When she went, she wasn't alone. She was accompanied by your love and the love in this room," Cole stated.

"It wasn't enough." Peter shook his head in disgust.

"Peter, we all pass on. Unfortunately, many of us, too many, pass on without having anyone to love them the way you loved your Sofia," Yossi added having picked up on Cole's theme.

"Love is the greatest gift," Rev. Hasbro said.

"I'm no good without her," Peter declared.

Yossi arranged for an ambulance to come pick up the deceased as Peter pulled himself together long enough to call relatives on his cell to break the news to them. Within a couple of minutes, the friend from across the street brought Peter's daughter over.

The friend looked at the strangers with Peter, took a quick glance at Sofia lifeless body then quickly told Peter how sorry he was for his loss before going back to his own flat before the police arrived.

"This is my daughter, Aleta."

Peter looked down at his daughter and sniffling said, "Aleta, say hello to the nice gentlemen? These men were with the Teguash."

Aleta sheepishly glanced at them, put her finger in her mouth then looked over her shoulder at her mother's corpse.

Peter led her to the mattress. In a low tone in her ear, he said, "Your mother is gone now. Take a last look and never forget. Never forget she loved you."

Aleta was frightened and clung to her father's arm for comfort.

"An ambulance will be here shortly. Maybe we should take the child back downstairs?" Yossi suggested.

"Yes, you take her," Peter said thrusting the child at Cole.

"You come too." Cole was disturbed by Peter's behavior.

"No, I want to be with her," Peter replied looking at his wife.

"You take my child. You take care of her. She is yours now," Peter declared.

Cole was flabbergasted by the implications of what Peter was suggesting and in his head a quick prayer went off, "God, don't let this go down this way."

"I can't raise her. It is only a matter of time before I end up like this," Peter reasoned.

"Not necessarily. There are medicines," Yossi tried to assure him.

"And how do I pay for them?" Peter asked in earnest.

"Maybe we know people who will help," Yossi suggested.

Cole agreed, "Yossi is right. We have a lot of contacts."

Peter just shook his head. "I'm no good without my Sofia. She was the only part of me that was alive."

"You need some time. Come downstairs with us," Yossi encouraged.

"No, you take the child. I will wait here for the ambulance," Peter said.

By the time the ambulance arrived, a small crowd had gathered outside the building. There were a few relatives and friends as word spread but there were also a handful of curiosity seekers with little respect for the moment.

Yossi talked to one of the medics who arrived. It was someone he'd worked with at his hospital's emergency room. Yossi filled him in on the situation.

"I wonder what will happen to them?" Rev. Hasbro asked.

Cole looked down at Aleta who reached up and held his hand. He wondered what kind of government help Peter would get in raising her. He looked around at the crowd.

There was a sizable Ethiopian community here. He'd at least have moral support.

"I don't know. I really don't know. The world is a messed up place, Bill," Cole replied.

There was a sudden shatter from above and the sound of glass could be heard landing on trash bins and vehicles along the street. Before Cole could look up to spot the source of the noise, there was a thud a few feet away.

"Oh, my," Rev. Hasbro uttered.

Cole looked over and in horror spotted Peter on the pavement. His head was smashed open and blood was running onto the street. The legs were bent in an awkward position. The expression on the face was one of bewilderment. Peter's body twitched a couple of times before falling still altogether.

From the window above from which Peter exited this world, a medic hung over the ledge. Seconds too late in stopping Peter, he was processing the failure that'd stick with him the rest of his life.

Some in the crowd screamed while others reverberated the sounds of startlement. Rev. Hasbro walked over and uttered a small prayer. It was never good for a disturbed soul to leave this earth alone, he thought.

Cole glanced down at Aleta whose jaw had dropped. Her eyes were like round saucers. He picked her up, holding her with her back to the scene.

It was after both bodies were loaded into the ambulance that a police officer came to take the child from Cole. She was reluctant to go but Cole was in little position to do otherwise. Besides, in the long run, he reasoned it was for the best.

The three men hailed a cab and left the scene without saying a word the rest of the way.

.   .   .   .

"Where did you go?" Monique asked as Cole returned to the hotel room. Cole didn't answer so Monique ignored his silence. "Well, you missed all the excitement. Have I got a story for you, remember that lady I told you about, the one with the baby up at Caesarea?"

A distant stare from Cole put Monique off a bit so she changed her tone.

"Well, you don't seem too interested in what happened to your wife today. I got injured you know."

Cole glanced her over, "Are you ok?"

"Depends, are you going to ignore me if I say 'yes'?" Monique teased.

Cole turned away and looked out the hotel window at the traffic down below.

Monique was becoming worried. "You aren't upset over the conversation about the baby we had, are you?"

"No. In fact, I'm glad you brought it up." Cole coldly stared out the window at nothing in particular.

Monique was taken back. "You are?"

"Bill and I ran into Yossi today," Cole told her.

"Yossi's in Tel Aviv? Wow! Guess it is a small world after all," Monique replied.

"We were at this Ethiopian restaurant …" Cole started.

"You ate already? Oh, honey!" Monique was disappointed. She'd hoped for a nice dinner together.

Cole continued, "A waiter there recognized us from Ethiopia."

"Ok, wow! I guess I was right the first time. It is a small world."

"His wife was sick. We went …" His voice trailed off at that point because no matter how badly he wished to tell Monique what had happened, he couldn't continue.

Monique slowly approached him. "Cole, are you ok?"

Cole broke his stare outside and reaching out, he wrapped Monique up into a giant hug. For a second she wasn't sure he was going to let go.

"What happened?" she asked.

"Love and life. That's what happened. Love and life," he said while refusing to loosen his grip.

CHAPTER 13: The Beach

Lady Marina stood at the wooden kitchen table, staring down at little Katrina who out of wonderment was gazing back up at her from her basket which had become a fixture in both their lives although Lady Marina was beginning to realize that in a few days the basket would be too small to serve its purpose.

"How strange this world must seem to you." Katrina only wiggled her little legs in response.

Lady Marina glanced at her watch. "Time to go, girlie."

She double-checked to make sure she had both sets of keys and that extra diapers were stuffed into the side of the basket. Yesterday, Lady Marina had run out of them and whew, if the smell wasn't a killer in the Israeli summer heat then she'd never met one. Actually, she had met a killer while out buying more diapers at the local AM/PM.

"Well, look who it is," Guy said.

Lady Marina instinctively pulled Katrina's basket closer.

"She's so cute." Guy leaned over to make a face to the baby.

"And from the smell of it, she is the reason you're here," he remarked, turning his nose away.

"It comes with having a baby in tow. But somehow, I'm not surprised you don't know that," Lady Marina sniped.

"True. Still, a little hard on the nostrils don't you think?"

"What do you want, Guy?"

"What's the matter? Suddenly, you're not happy to see me? Maybe, I just want to invite you for more pizza. Anything wrong with that?"

"No, if that was the reason you're here but it's not," she replied.

Lady Marina took her free hand and reached inside a back pocket for a small knife hidden there. Her fingers grasped the handle.

"Relax," Guy said detecting the movement.

"If pizza was all you wanted, you would've called," Lady Marina pointed out.

"I never could get anything past you, could I?" Guy sarcastically agreed.

"So, like I said, what do you want?" Lady Marina repeated.

"Well, I was going to come by your place but as I was going by I saw you duck in here and thought this would be a better place for us to speak," he explained.

"You were following me, weren't you? Weren't you?" She was alarmed by the prospect.

Guy bobbled his head as though he didn't want to admit tailing her.

"Why?"

"Yuri."

"I just saw Yuri, yesterday," Lady Marina said.

"You saw Yuri with a tail and a stray baby you picked up in an alley somewhere. The tail is bad for business and in Yuri's line of work you really don't want uninvited visitors."

Lady Marina glanced around to map out an escape route.

"I told you to relax," Guy instructed.

"Easy for you to say."

"If I wanted anything other than talk, do you think we'd be standing here like this? Yuri just wants to find out if there is a reason you were being adored by others from afar. I told him it was your charm."

Lady Marina released the grip on her knife but not on baby Katrina's basket.

"Now see, the baby is another matter. Don't get me wrong. I'm not a monster. I like kids."

Guy bent down and said, "Goochy goochy goo." To Katrina who peered on with indifference.

He continued, "But Yuri is another matter. He considers the kid, well, let's say a distraction."

"A distraction?"

"How can you concentrate on business at hand if you're busy changing diapers? Yuri is willing to take the kid off your hands," Guy explained.

"Which is why you're here." Lady Marina surmised.

"Exactly. But, I know you're attached to the kid, and well, let's face it, who'd want to leave their baby with Yuri, right?"

"Not me." Lady Marina sounded rather determined in her answer.

Guy agreed, "Me, either."

"What are you suggesting?" Lady Marina asked.

"That we never had this conversation."

"Understood."

"Do you know where you'll take her?" Guy asked.

"Some place safe."

Lady Marina had always followed a policy of allotting herself the option of being able to run on a moment's notice. The extra set of keys stuffed in her pocket were for a flat across town. The one room accommodation was located in a back alley attracting few visitors and zero attention. Until now, she'd only gone there every couple of weeks to check that it was secure.

"Some place safe is good," Guy agreed.

"What will you tell, Yuri?" Lady Marina asked.

"I'll tell him you weren't home which as it turns out is true," Guy answered with a smile.

He turned and started walking down the aisle before pausing. Turning back around he said, "Call me when you get free to go for pizza."

"I'll do that," Lady Marina promised.

Lady Marina hurried around the store, bought all the goods she needed and that she could carry along with the baby. She scurried to the nearest bus stop where she put Katrina down on a bench. Looking like any other commuter, she scoped the street. Seeing no one suspicious, she picked Katrina back up and walked around the nearest corner where her jeep was parked.

.   .   .   .

The girl in the green shirt rubbed her eyes. Her head resting on a purple backpack covered in band stickers. The last two days of her life had turned into a blur. It'd been a frenzy of bouncing from flat to flat, partying with various friends which had worn her young body down.

She peeked over at her boyfriend stretched out on the couch. His boot laces were undone at the top. Seeing his mouth cracked opened on one side, she tapped her mp3 player, grateful she wasn't listening to his snoring.

A smile crossed her face. The dye job on his mohawk looked really, really, cool. Crimson red was her ideal. He needed a little sprucing up to stand out in the crowd.

Even though he was two years older than her 15, she felt at times she was the mature one. He just needed her touch occasionally to keep him balanced in life.

She hated guessing what life was going to be like without him when he went into the army next year. She supposed that would be the end of them. Their paths would be making a permanent divergence at that point. Everything has an end. Couples. School. Governments. Even this day and the whole partying week would grind to a halt and they'd all turn back into pumpkins with the clock's striking of 12. She scooted herself up before reaching for a nearby bottle of wine and taking a swig.

Her head bobbed a couple of times with the classic tunes of *The Clash.* For old stuff, *London Calling* was really, really good. Reaching behind her, she grabbed an electric

Gibson she'd stumbled upon in a pawn shop off Allenby St. for a ridiculously low price. She'd lifted some money from her aunt to help pay for it. The beau had a deal going down shortly that promised to let her pay the aunt back before the money was missed.

Strumming along with the music, she corrected herself a couple of times after hitting the wrong notes. She longed to join a band. The dream was to bring some serious rock-n-roll to Tel Aviv. Lord knows, the city needed it.

A pillow smacked her upside the head. She picked it up and threw it back at her boyfriend who dodged it as it sailed by.

"Quit making all that racket," he said while looking around for the pack of cigarettes he was sure he'd had before falling asleep.

She pulled the headphones out, "What?"

"Quit making all that racket. You can't play guitar anyway," he said.

She picked up the pack of cigarettes laying nearby that he was looking for and tossed it to him. "Yes, I can to play."

"No, you can't."

"Well, I'm learning anyway."

He looked at her blankly for a second before admitting, "Yeah, I guess you have picked-up a few chords."

This concession made her smile. "See, you know I'm going to be a star someday but don't worry, you'll be in my entourage," she joked.

"Entourage? Really? Well that's generous of you," he teased.

"I think so."

He looked down at his watch. "We have to go."

She put the guitar back in its place and started gathering up her gear.

"Do you need to call your parents? Because no phone calls while I'm doing this thing, understood?"

She shook her head, "Nah. They're at work besides they'd just ask what I was up too and I'd prefer not to lie."

"Come on then." With that the lovebirds left the flat for the bus stop two blocks up the street.

.   .   .   .

The sound of the waves hit Monique's ears with a tranquility she rarely experienced back home in St. Clair. Between the call center, Eric and of course Cole, real life tranquility was non-existent. Here though on Dolphin Beach Monique was basking in the sun leaving the rest of the world, except for Cole who was laying a few feet from her, planets away.

The waves resonated like a car zooming by on an isolated road on a far away island. She was impervious to the grains of sand being swept out to sea that were eroding the ground beneath where she rested. She reached for a tube of sunscreen near the blanket but Cole beat her to it and so Monique rolled over to let him do his devotional duty.

"You're getting pretty tanned," Cole observed as he rubbed the lotion into her back.

"Good," Monique stated with a grin.

"I wish it could be like this every day," Cole said looking out across the Mediterranean.

"You still thinking about last night?" Monique asked.

"Of course."

Monique reached up and kissed him. "Don't fret about what you have no control over."

"Aren't you the meditative one," Cole responded.

"Maybe. But I know you couldn't have helped either of those people."

Cole sat back in the sand. "I know, but if you could've seen it. Well, actually I'm glad you didn't."

"Look, the lady was, for all intents and purposes dead when you arrived and you had no way of knowing the guy was going to toss himself out a window. How could you?"

"I know." Cole had tried to convince himself of the same thing a thousand times since last night. His head knew it but it didn't make it any easier for his heart to bear. "Still, if you could've seen that little girl."

"Come on, honey. What could you do? They weren't going to let you take her home. I mean, you didn't want to take her home did you?"

Cole paused a second.

"Not really. I just wanted to help."

There was a second pause.

"Would it have bothered you if I did bring her home?" Cole inquired.

Monique rolled over onto her side. "I thought I was the one who was giving having another child consideration."

"You don't have to make it sound so businesslike," Cole said.

"You want to adopt? Is that what you're trying to tell me?" Monique asked.

"Maybe we could do both," Cole said shrugging his shoulders.

Monique broke out in laughter.

"It's not that funny."

"Yes, it is. Trust me, it is. You went from doubting if you want any more children to having two more? Tell me that isn't funny," Monique replied.

"I'm just thinking if we can help a kid like that, we'd be doing our part to make the world a bit of a better place," Cole replied.

"Well, remember you're saving the world when doing all the diaper changes. Look, even if we could adopt, you won't be able to help that little girl. I'm sure there are laws. It's not that easy. So you'd better have a better reason than that before you dive head first into something like this," Monique declared.

"You're right."

"As usual," Monique teased.

Cole stretched out on the sand. He just needed to relax. The emotions of the last 24 hours would dissipate if he gave them a chance.

Monique leaned over and kissed him.

"You have a good heart, Dr. Time. That's one reason I married you. At any rate, life seems more manageable from this spot right here," Monique told him.

"You should listen to me more often," Cole joked.

Monique hushed him. "You're interfering with the sound of the tide."

Shifting his sunglasses into better position, Cole wondered why the universe consisted of so many contradictions. There was to be no walking on water today just a contemplative nature of how souls are set adrift, cast into the deep blue where the tide tosses them, looking to be chartered into the hinterlands of the universe.

The haunting voice had spoken of love. Cole pictured what it was to love. Philosophical deliberations weren't his forte but history was and if history demonstrated anything it was that there was no force as powerful as love. Before Cole knew it, he was in a comfort zone as the tension that'd been pent up eroded with the tide.

He could feel himself walking along the dirt lots where he and the neighborhood kids played ball when he was young. He'd hung out in those run down parks from noon to sundown during summer vacations.

There was the grass beneath his feet as he climbed the hill where an old burned down house on the edge of town lay in ruins. It'd been a farm house at one point and being off the main road, no one had rebuilt it.

Cole use to ride his bike out there and climb the hill where the house had once served as a sentinel tower over the farm. He dug around, dreaming of discovering a hidden treasure he imagined the former owners had abandoned in the midst of their tragedy.

For all his archaeological troubles, Cole ended up with a couple old canning jars, shreds of old newspapers eaten away by the elements, and a razor that'd fallen into the dirt.

Home, now there was love. Monique and that look she gave him when he knew it was going to be ok come what may.

"Hey, stop!!!! Cole! Cole!"

It took a second for Monique's voice to sink into his consciousness but when it did, Cole snapped out of his daydreaming and sat up with a start. She was pointing at a teenager sprinting across the sand. He was getting better traction since he was barefoot. He was making a beeline for the nearby boardwalk.

"He stole my bag!" Monique shouted. Cole jumped up and took after the thief who had a good head start on him.

Thirty seconds into the chase, Cole realized that running in sand looked easier than it really was. There was probably a reason he only saw people do this on television and not too often on the beach itself.

He saw the thief glance back apparently surprised Cole was still in pursuit. The thief ran past a small monument to teenagers who'd been victims in one of Tel Aviv's worse suicide attacks in history and pulled up at the sidewalk. As Cole was to find out, running barefoot in the sand is one thing but doing it on pavement in the Middle East heat was quite another matter especially when you weren't use to it. Panting and amazed by how out of shape one teacher from Indiana could be, the heat on his feet actually helped speed him up. Like stepping on hot coals, the best advice was to keep moving. Behind him, a couple men had also joined the chase in an effort to aid Cole.

The number 10 bus was rolling through the normal beach front traffic congestion. The road construction underway in the Yafo part of the city wasn't helping. The driver wondered to himself what it would be like once the light rail system was in place. Probably only add to the problem he sarcastically figured.

The driver looked up in the mirror. A drunk had decided to entertain everyone with a slurred version of *Soul Man*. Passengers were trying to move aside, ignoring the irritation, as the man walked further toward the back.

"I'm a Soul Man! Yes, I am," the man belted out giving the girl in green a blast of vodka laced breath that caused the hair in her nostrils curl.

"You also can't sing on key," the girl in the green shot back.

The drunk tapped the guitar case, the girl had slung around her shoulder.

"Hey! Hands off the guitar," she warned.

"Ah, maybe, if you played along I would sound even better than I do," the man suggested.

"Nothing would make you sound good but a breath mint would be a good start," the girl retorted bringing chuckles from nearby passengers.

"Hey, don't get sassy with me," the man's tone turned angry.

The girl's boyfriend stepped toward the guy, "Back off, jerk."

Seeing the situation deteriorating, the girl intervened by putting her hand on her boyfriend's chest. "It's ok, baby. Remember, you have that thing to take care of."

"Yeah, better listen to your little girlfriend. Take care of that thing," the drunk laughingly mocked.

The girl reached up and gave her boyfriend a long passionate kiss before he could retort. The public display of affection didn't bother her. She didn't care if the world approved or not.

"Hey, how about one of those me?" the drunk asked. The girl finally broke off her kiss and just looked at the drunk with a *you wish* glare.

"I am the Soul Man after all!" the drunk shouted at the top of his lungs.

The girl in green just leaned her head on her boyfriend's chest in defiance.

"Come on, one for the Soul Man?" The drunk leaned over to try and kiss the girl who quickly jerked her head to away.

The boyfriend pushed the drunk back against side of the bus.

"Hey, you can't do that to the Soul Man," the drunk shouted as he lunged at the boyfriend who knocked him to the floor.

The boyfriend took a couple shots at the drunk to keep him on the floor and the girl in green managed to get in a kick to the side of his face. She figured she was owed one good shot just for the aggravation.

The scuffle brought shouts from the fellow passengers who while annoyed by the Soul Man didn't want a full-scale brawl to occur either. No one was jumping in to break it up, after all the drunk was the one sprawled out on the floor, but the cries to stop grew louder.

Hearing the howls of the passengers, the driver looked up into his mirror. Now what? He thought he could see a scuffle of some sort but if no one was getting killed then he could wait until the next stop to throw that drunk off the bus and radio for the police to pick him up.

"Stop that back there!" the driver warned without results.

He turned on his address system. "I said stop that back there. I'm going to throw you off!"

The driver shook his head in disgust seeing his warning carried no authority. He turned his attention back to the road. A teenager carrying a bag came running off the sidewalk straight into traffic just yards ahead of him.

The breaks squealing on the bus could be heard up and down the street. The bus jolted sending the combatants in the back sprawling across the floor. Other passengers were grabbing for whatever they could latch on too.

Realizing he wasn't going to be able to miss the teenager, the driver yanked the wheel hard to the left in an effort to swerve and give some distance. If the teenager reacted as well, they just might miss each other.

It was such a gut reaction that the driver didn't have time to weigh out the consequences of what he was doing. No sooner had the bus started to cross the lanes than it slammed straight into a jeep passing it from the side.

Lady Marina had been speeding along the road she traveled daily. The tunes were going and she was reminding herself that whatever happened with Yuri or Guy, she was the one in control.

She smiled down at Katrina who seemed content in her little basket. Lady Marina gave her a little tickle before out of the corner of her eye she noticed the bus she was passing turn straight into her. Instinctively, she clutched Katrina and held her grip for dear life.

The jeep, for all its ruggedness, was no match for the looming bus barreling into it. The jeep was immediately flipped over onto its side and pushed into oncoming traffic where two cars plowed into it, spinning it around like a top.

Caught in a dizzying spin, Lady Marina felt her grip on the wheel broken as the jeep slid into the other lane. With the impact of the first car from the other lane, she saw the jeep spin away from her and felt the burn of the pavement beneath her back. She started to look for Katrina but her vision blacked out and while there was a sensation of what was happening to her, she couldn't see it.

The teenage thief who'd started the tragic chain reaction had seen the bus bearing down on him and froze. It was his first glimpse of death and unfortunately, death was staring back.

Wide-eyed, petrified to the point where every thought froze in is brain, the thief stood in the roadway and watched as the front of the bus swerved. He saw it broadside the jeep and slam it into the other lane. The sound of the metal meshing was still ringing in his ears as he turned his head back in time to see the tail of the bus inches away from his body.

Cole stopped in his tracks as he saw the thief's body disappear and the bus skid over the spot where he'd been standing. Somehow, the force of the impact propelled Monique's bag back toward the sidewalk where it landed spreading the contents out onto the ground.

Cole gathered up some of Monique's possessions, especially her wallet. He glanced over at the crash scene. He could see a bloody lump, the teenage thief's mangled body that'd been scooped up by the side of the bus and was now laying heaped on the underside of the carriage.

Traffic was at a halt. People exited their cars seemingly with everyone on a cellphone telling their version of what happened. The guys, who'd been giving chase with Cole, went over and looked at the thief's body, shaking their heads at the tragedy.

Monique came running up as well.

"Are you all right?" she asked before getting a glimpse of the thief.

She turned her head into Cole. "Oh, my God."

Cole handed her the bag and said, "Hold this. Stay here. I'm going to check and see if there are others hurt.

Inside the bus, the driver had banged his head against the steering wheel when he collided with the jeep. He shook the bells ringing in his head, peeked into his side mirror and saw the overturned jeep surrounded by the wrecked cars which had smashed into it. Looking on the other side, the kid who'd been standing in the road was nowhere to be seen.

"Whoa that was a near miss," the driver thought to himself.

Reaching for the radio, the driver put in the emergency call to the office. He could tell others were placing calls as well. It'd be only minutes before emergency crews arrived on the scene.

His passengers were shaken up badly by what had happened. There were even a couple not so friendly gestures directed at him but he didn't have time to argue now.

Getting on the public address system, he issued his instructions, "Everyone, listen. Listen to me. Stay calm and check the person next to you. Make sure the person you are next to is not hurt. If you are hurt, please, let someone know."

He paused as there was a buzz while everyone checked their neighbor and expressed their gratitude at having survived the ordeal. Then the gasp and scream he'd feared occurred.

The boyfriend rolled off the drunk, moaning, having smashed his head against the floor as he tumbled forward.

For his part, the drunk staggered up, saying, "I'm a Soul Man. Yes, I am. Soul Man," though the only person listening at this point was himself.

The boyfriend knew immediately he was going to have to be swallowing a bottle of aspirin. He crawled up and noticed the girl in green sprawled out on the floor, her guitar wedged behind her back and a dark red stain spreading onto the filthy floor. A lady in a nearby seat let out a scream.

"Babe? Babe!" The boyfriend crawled over to her not knowing the best way to pick her up. The girl was conscious though her eyes spoke of pain.

"I think I'm hurt. Sorry, looks like we'll be late for that thing," she said trying to force a smile that never came.

She'd been standing, holding onto the metal frame when the collision occurred. The force had thrown her small frame up against the metal snapping the guitar slung behind her and in the thrusting back and forth of the wreck, the snapped head of the guitar had been lodged into her back.

"I've got to roll you on your side, ok?" the boyfriend explained. The girl in green bit her lip and braced herself as the turn came.

The boyfriend could see the guitar lodged into her back. He was contemplating how best to pull it out when a soldier who'd stepped forward to help, warned, "Best not try it. You could damage organs if you yank it out wrong."

"Babe …"

"It's ok," the girl mumbled.

"I'll get you a new guitar, ok?" the boyfriend promised but he never got an answer as the light that lived in her eyes and which he'd always taken for granted suddenly was extinguished.

Outside, Cole made his way to the other side of the bus where a crowd was gathering around a jeep. As he neared the wreck he spied a lady on the ground clutching what looked like a baby to her chest the way a football player might cling to the ball as he got hammered crossing the goal line.

Lady Marina heard a jumbo of voices around her. She could feel pain shooting up her spine. The sight which had temporarily disappeared was now returning and as she struggled to focus she saw a man with a bushy mustache leaning over trying check her body. Then she felt a second person trying to slide a crying Katrina away from her body.

It took a tremendous effort, and she had to bite down on the pain, but she managed with her free hand to reach the sling blade she had stashed in her pocket. When she whipped it out the men quickly retreated.

"Let her lay there. If she wants to die, let her," one man declared.

Someone else replied, "Yeah, but the baby?"

Another face coming into view made her raise the knife as a warning but the features were more familiar.

"Lady Marina? Lady Marina is that you?" Cole asked astonished to find his old acquaintance here and in this condition.

"Cole Tarkington," Lady Marina struggled with the words.

"It's been a long time," Cole said glancing over at the baby who seemed ok upon first glance.

"Yeah, well, Ethiopia was a ways ago, know what I mean?" Lady Marina said in a raspy tone.

236

Cole could hear sirens in the background closing in fast.

"I think I know exactly what you mean," he said

"Looks like I messed up this time," Lady Marina concluded as she winced from the pain.

"Accidents happen. An ambulance is on the way," Cole assured her.

"And the police I suppose?"

"Probably," Cole told her.

"We don't always get along. The police and I," Lady Marina explained.

"Do you want me to take the baby?" Cole started to reach for the child but she tightened her grip and flashed the blade one more time.

"What do you know about babies?" Lady Marina asked.

"Quite a bit, actually," Monique said as she bent down near the child. Lady Marina held the knife up but Cole pulled her arm back and took it away.

"This is my wife," Cole explained.

"You're married? Well, even losers get lucky," Lady Marina gave a coughing laugh. Cole noticed a trickle of blood escaping the corner of her mouth.

"I guess they do," Cole responded.

Lady Marina released her grip on a wailing Katrina and motioned for Monique to take her which she gently did.

237

Monique gave the baby a quick examination and miraculously discovered she was uninjured.

Monique gave a sigh of relief.

"Take her," Lady Marina said.

"What?" Cole asked.

"Take her. She isn't safe." It hurt for Lady Marina to get the words out.

Cole was confused. "What do you mean?"

Lady Marina grimaced, "You know the type of people I work for. She isn't safe."

Cole saw the first ambulance and police vehicles pulling up.

"Take the baby and I will meet you at the hotel room, understood?" Cole instructed Monique who complied before the police arrived.

. . . .

Yossi was ready in the emergency room when the ambulances started arriving. Word was most of the injuries were light but that there had been two fatalities on the scene of the accident.

Yossi was prepared for the worse. This was what an emergency room doctor trains for. It was now that his best was expected. Still, he was caught off guard when he saw Cole walk through the doors with paramedics.

"Are you ok?" he said rushing over to Cole.

"Yeah. I'm fine," Cole assured him.

"Doc," a paramedic motioned to a gurney.

Yossi received a double shock, "Lady Marina?"

"Did I get knocked back to Addis Ababa or something?" Lady Marina complained.

"No, I can assure you that you're still Tel Aviv," Yossi replied.

"Well, at least I got a doctor I know," Lady Marina said.

Yossi got vital stats from the paramedics and began checking Lady Marina.

"How bad?" she painfully asked.

"Bad enough. Guess I'm going to have to earn my pay today," Yossi answered before ordering a nearby nurse to get an operating room ready.

Lady Marina looked at Cole, "Promise to take care of baby Katrina?"

"Who is baby Katrina?" Yossi asked.

"I promise," Cole told her.

"Who is ..." Cole made a motion for Yossi to stop so the doctor motioned for the staff to wheel Lady Marina on back into the operating arena.

"There is a baby involved," Cole whispered.

"Is it ok?" Yossi inquired.

"Monique has it," Cole explained.

"I don't know that, ok?"

"Understood," Cole said.

"Go. I will catch up to you at the hotel when this over," Yossi instructed.

.   .   .   .

In an office where the well-dressed secretary at the front desk with the window view of the city gave Yuri's business the air of legitimacy, Guy was trying to keep a lid on matters. "I don't know where she is," he explained to Yuri.

"Lady Marina. Ha! What is that gutter trash up too?" Yuri demanded.

"How do I know? I mean, does anyone ever know what she is up too?" Guy replied.

Yuri stared at Guy for a second but there was no reason to think Guy would cover for that troublemaker. There was no gain to it.

Guy's cellphone rang and he reached into his pocket to answer, "Hello." There was a pause as he listened to news from the other end.

"I see. I will take care of it." Guy shut off the phone and slid it back into his pocket.

"I have to go," Guy said heading to the door.

Now, Yuri was suspicious.

Guy continued, "Might have a lead on Lady Marina."

"In that case, go. Get that scoundrel and bring her here," Yuri ordered.

"And the baby?"

Yuri shrugged. "Not my problem. Don't make it yours. Understood?"

Guy left the room glad his days with Yuri were numbered.

.   .   .   .

Guy stopped a nurse rushing through the ER.

"Admittance is that way." Lihi pointed in the opposite direction.

"No, I am looking for someone. You have had her in surgery. She was in the bus accident," Guy explained.

"And you are?" Lihi didn't like the looks of the guy. Something about him she didn't trust and she had a pretty good track record of sniffing out those of less than redeemable qualities.

Guy reached into his pocket withdrawing his identification which he flashed in front of the nurse.

"I see. Shouldn't you talk to administration first?" Lihi asked.

"The patient," Guy was growing agitated.

Lihi led Guy into a recovery room where Yossi was checking out a drugged up Lady Marina who was slowly regaining her senses after the operation.

"Dr. Peer. This gentleman wishes to see the patient," Lihi said.

"Who are you?" Yossi asked.

"Guy?" Lady Marina mumbled.

"Friend of the family, I see." Yossi motioned for Lihi to leave.

"Not really," Guy replied as he passed Yossi his identification.

"Ah, Shin Bet. No, I guess you aren't friends of the family after all." Yossi handed the identification back.

Lady Marina let out a strange, almost insane sounding laugh, "Sleeping with the enemy."

"She's still a little loopy from the operation," Yossi explained.

"You don't seem surprised to see me," Guy concluded.

"I just can't figure out what Israel's domestic spy agency could find interesting about a bus crash," Yossi stated.

"I want to question your patient for a moment," Guy explained.

"I can't consent to that," Yossi replied.

"I do it here or I have her hauled, just as she is, down to headquarters," Guy warned.

"It's ok," Lady Marina mumbled.

Yossi stepped out of the room feeling torn up about leaving a vulnerable Lady Marina at the mercy of Shin Bet. She may not have the clean background one would like but he'd always gotten the impression she was more a victim of circumstance than a heartless thug.

"Come to arrest me?" Lady Marina joked at Guy.

"Not if I can help it," Guy answered.

"You on the take? You going to hand me over to Yuri?" Lady Marina was less joking at this point. It was rare for Shin Bet to be on the take but the police was rife with corruption. People like Yuri wouldn't flourish otherwise.

"Well, he's looking for you," Guy informed her.

"I can handle him," Lady Marina swore.

"Really?" Guy reached over to a bandaged area where Yossi had clearly done some work and put a slight bit of pressure on it. Lady Marina started to let out a yelp but bit her tongue.

"See, I don't think you're quite your normal self. But tell you what. I will help you if you help me."

"Why should I help you?" Lady Marina asked.

"Because you want to live," Guy replied.

There was a pause before Lady Marina asked, "What do you want?"

Guy explained how he'd make her disappear if she would agree to testify. It was her chance for a new start. She'd be starting from the bottom but it'd be a new start all the same. Guy even promised to make sure she got back to her home in the Ukraine if that is where she wanted to go.

"Doctor!" Guy yelled prompting Yossi to rush back into the room.

"This is the official line. She died in this room right here, right now from complications," Guy declared.

"But …"

"No 'but' to it. Fill out the paperwork immediately and have it put into the system. Then get her placed in an isolated ward. Mark her as quarantined or something with an alias. No one is to see her but me and you. Understood?"

Yossi nodded that he got the plan but there was still one hitch. "My supervisor won't approve. All the paperwork I generate goes past his desk and he doesn't like me. He really doesn't like me," Yossi stressed.

"What's his name?"

"Dr. Ali Zarouk." Yossi answered.

"Arab?"

"Yes."

"That's easy enough. I'll take care of it," Guy promised.

Yossi didn't like the sound of that but even an Israeli would've been left with little choice.

"Quarantine within the next 15 minutes, oh and the baby, see if you can find someone who'll take care of it." With the commands issued, Guy winked at Lady Marina and exited the room.

In the hallway, Guy pulled out his phone and placed two calls. The first was to Yuri explaining that Lady Marina had been killed in a car accident. He figured Yuri would eventually find out about the accident anyway so it was best to be up front about it.

The second call was to his superiors at Shin Bet whom he informed him of Lady Marina's current predicament. He stressed to them that they now had a living witness and while there were precautions to take, it was time to close Yuri down.

Guy wasn't the only one who knew how to put his cellphone to good use. Yossi did what Guy ordered. He explained the situation to Lihi who entered Lady Marina's death information into the hospital record system. Anyone accessing it, such as an informant for Yuri, would discover how Lady Marina died from brain contusions suffered during the accident. Anyone looking at photos of the accident would believe that story.

Then Lihi and Yossi wheeled Lady Marina up to a special ward where she was checked in as Rachel Zorn, a tourist who'd contracted a contagious virus. Yossi had allowed Lady Marina to pick out her own alias. He figured she'd be less likely to make a slip-up that way. When he got a chance to be alone again, he made one other phone call.

"David, its Yossi. Listen, I need to speak with you urgently. Any chance you could drive up from Jerusalem?"

"I need to speak with you too. How does breakfast on the beach sound, in the morning?" David Landsberg suggested.

"Sounds like we have a plan," Yossi concurred.

.   .   .   .

Dr. Ali Zarouk was standing looking out his office window. He was tired. He wanted to go home and spend time with his family but the hospital was crammed. The bus accident had only doubled their normal work load.

There was a critical patient brought in that Yossi Peer was operating on. Dr. Zarouk supposed the patient was in good hands. Despite his insolent attitude, Dr. Peer did seem competent in the operating room. Still, he was about to go down and check for himself how things were proceeding.

His office door flew open and six men, all plains clothes but clearly armed entered the room.

"Dr. Ali Zarouk?" the leader inquired.

"Yes! What is the meaning of this?" Dr. Zarouk demanded.

The men flashed their identifications. "Shin Bet. We need you to come with us. We have questions we'd like to ask you. Informally, of course."

Dr. Ali Zarouk knew that if he went with these men it might be weeks before his family found out what happened to him.

"Can I call my wife?" Dr. Zarouk pleaded.

"Perhaps later," the leader replied knowing there'd be no phone calls for at least 72 hours.

Dr. Zarouk was paraded through the hospital corridors feeling like a criminal although he knew in his heart that'd done no crime. Still, his co-workers looked upon him with suspicion, whispering as he was marched past them.

Whatever the outcome of his interrogation, his future at the hospital was over.

CHAPTER 14: Picking Up The Pieces

The office was decked out with a collection of mementos from scattered places around the globe. A lucky stack of cards from Las Vegas. A House of Blues menu autographed by a female guitar player, which was only one token from an infamous night in Chicago. Carved wooden rhinos bought cheap from a shop in Nairobi and a badly crafted rosary from Puerto Prince.

David Landsberg wasn't sure why he kept the rosary. It possessed no spiritual value to him. He certainly was no fan of the Pope considering what had happened to his family during World War Two.

"Girlfriend?" the official from the Interior Minister's office asked, pointing at a picture of a dark-haired beauty sporting a tank top and pair of jeans that was sitting on a shelf near David's desk.

David spun his chair around then broke out in a chuckle, "I wish. Friend of a friend who is a television actress. She let me sit in on a taping of her show then gave me the picture afterward."

"Sounds like there's a story there," the official commented.

"There is," David said dropping the subject.

The Interior Minister's aide was understandably nervous. His boss didn't know he was visiting David and if word leaked out he was here then it would be his job. After all, his boss believed immigration shouldn't exist except for the most orthodox of the Orthodox. Everyone else should be barred and deported. David on the other hand was determined to help as many as he could and block unnecessary deportations.

Immigration was the reason the two were meeting now. They'd been military buddies and so when they were sharing a cup of coffee this morning and David was speaking of having to go to Yafo and check on a Dr. Yossi Peer, an alarm went off in the aide's head.

The name sounded familiar so while in the coffee shop, the aide had pulled out his smartphone and surfed through documents emailed to him. There buried, in the 200-plus arriving that morning, was the report on the immigrant who'd captured headlines by killing himself. The attached police report listed as a witness none other than Dr. Yossi Peer. The same Yossi Peer his army buddy had mentioned.

"What about the child? This Aleta? Where is she now?" David inquired.

"Protective services has her until the deportation paperwork is finished. Sometime next week, I imagine," the aide informed him.

"So you are going to deport her?"

"Yes," the aide confirmed.

"But it says here, the parents are Jewish," David observed.

"Well, the father is. No question about that. But it seems the mother had some questionable documents or lack of proof for her grandmother, I believe it is. After checking with the Rabbinate, the feeling is there is enough questions about her background to declare her non-Jewish and therefore the child isn't Jewish either."

"You take your orders from the Rabbinate?"

The aide shrugged, "The system is what it is."

"To do this to a child?"

"One less mouth for the State to feed," the aide commented.

"Do you really feel that way?" David asked.

"Look, her mother was obviously not religious. Her father had to be psycho and maybe the mother was too, who knows? The child is going to be messed up. Why shouldn't the State push it off on someone else?"

David was just gearing up to let loose his fury when his cell rang. It was Yossi on the other end wanting to meet with him. David quickly set the time and hung up.

"Can you give me 48 hours?" David asked.

"Sure. We're still waiting on the paperwork. But listen, David."

"Yeah?"

"I wouldn't stick my neck too far out on this one," the aide warned.

.   .   .   .

The window where Peter had launched himself to his death still wasn't fixed and from the looks of the neighborhood, David assumed it might be some time before a repairman made an appearance.

"He was a good guy. Tsk, tsk," a nearby fruit vendor commented. David had been having a hard time finding anyone who was willing to admit they knew Peter.

"So you knew him?" David inquired.

"Sure. Well, I knew him as well as any of my other customers I suppose. I mean he and that wife of his stopped here two or three times a week. Of course when she became

252

ill, I guess he stopped by less regularly," the vendor said trying to recall exactly how often they did stop by.

"So his wife's illness really affected him?"

"Wouldn't your wife falling ill like that affect you?" the vendor retorted with a tinge of sarcasm.

"Did they go to synagogue?" David inquired.

"What do you need to know that for?" the vendor suspiciously asked.

"I'm trying to help the daughter," David explained.

"Well, Peter worked so hard I doubt he had time for it. Besides, our people aren't exactly welcomed in most synagogues around here," the vendor's resentment seeped into his voice.

"Where did his wife work before she became ill?"

"She was a maid for a while," the vendor volunteered.

"I saw that in the records. What I was wondering was, where she worked that made her ill?"

The vendor looked around to make sure no one was watching then pointed to a connecting street. "Take a right and look for the sign."

The neon sign wasn't hard to spot. It was cheap like the atmosphere. David went through the curtain that passed as a door and down a flight of rickety steps that ended in a lobby where he was greeted by three women dressed scantly like caricatures out of a bad private eye dime novel.

The air itself was musty and David felt like he was in a dungeon of despair. He was aware there were scores of brothels in Tel Aviv and this was typical fare. One of the women rose from her chair to greet him but he stopped her and quickly got to his business before she started to pitch hers.

"I'm wanting to find out about Sophia," David informed her.

The women remained in mute mode until one finally piped up, "You aren't police?"

"No. I'm a lawyer trying to help her daughter, Aleta. They want to send her back to Ethiopia."

"They'd do that?" another lady asked.

"What do you think?" David responded.

"She loved that girl. It was the reason she was here. They trusted the wrong people, if you know what I mean." The girl looked around as though afraid the wrong person might overhear her.

A customer came down the stairs.

"That confirms what I'd guessed." David pulled out two hundred shekels from his pocket which he handed to the girl who'd given him the information.

"That goes to you, not your boss. If you can, get away from this place," David warned before heading back up the stairs. He had one more stop before calling it a night.

The Lieberman's house was in a nicer area of North Tel Aviv. By Israeli standards, it was upper middle class and though it was quiet when David arrived, he sensed children kept the house hopping. Though on short notice, the Lieberman's agreed to talk to David for a few minutes.

"How long did Sophia work for you?" David asked.

"Um, six months I think," Mrs. Lieberman answered.

"I couldn't believe what happened to them. When you told us that, I was in shock. It's a strange world," Mr. Lieberman said.

"Why'd you let her go?"

"We didn't have a choice. She missed almost two weeks of work in a row. I mean, we hired her to help with the children. With our jobs, it is so difficult," Mrs. Lieberman answered.

"Two weeks? Did she say why?"

"Something about her daughter being sick. Some kind of fever but I don't know if that was really the case. I wasn't even sure if she had a daughter," Mrs. Lieberman explained.

"She worked here six months and you aren't sure if she had a daughter?" David was astounded and somewhat offended by Mrs. Lieberman's attitude.

Mr. Lieberman tried to come to his wife's defense, "Well, we never saw any of the family so there was no way for us to know for sure."

"Sophia did have a daughter. Now they want to deport her," David informed them.

"On what grounds?" Mr. Lieberman asked.

"Turns out now they are questioning Sophia's Jewishness," David replied.

"Well, I'm not surprised," Mrs. Lieberman stated.

"Why not?"

"I got the feeling she never went to services on Shabbat. You know some of those people should never be let into the country in the first place. Especially, if she has AIDS. What if she had exposed us to it?" Mrs. Lieberman shuddered at the thought.

David stood up and headed to the door. "For your information, she got the disease working in a brothel after you fired her. Next time you make your once a year pilgrimage to synagogue during the High Holy Days, you might include firing underpaid maids in your list of sins."

. . . .

Cole and Rev. Hasbro spent a good deal of the day learning which stores near the hotel carried items for baby care. The hotel staff had been helpful in pointing them in the right direction.

It seemed though each time they returned to the hotel room, Monique had a new list ready and was saying, "And we'll need this and that." Finally, when the two men returned from the last trip, they were ready to collapse.

Cole sat slumped in a chair as Monique held Katrina. She hadn't let the baby out of her sight since leaving the hospital. As far as Monique was concerned, she was a miracle baby, something precious deserving to be nurtured.

"It's not such a bad idea," Monique remarked.

"What isn't?"

"This," she replied indicating the baby.

"No, I guess not." Cole realized no matter how this turned out the prospect of a second child was going to be subject for discussion for a period to come.

"Do you want to hold her?" Monique asked.

"No, I just want to sit," Cole said.

There was a knock at the door and Cole sighed as he got up to answer it. A power nap would be welcomed right now, he thought.

He never got the door all the way opened before Sis. Gladys managed to barge on in with a hideous looking scarf purchased at the Carmiel Market.

"I just couldn't wait to show you the bargain of the day! What do you think?" Sis. Gladys spun around as though she was on a catwalk in New York.

"Ssshh," Cole and Monique said in unison but it was followed by a slight wail from Katrina.

"Did she wake you up? I'm sorry," Monique said placating Katrina.

Sis. Gladys pointed at Katrina, "That's a baby."

"Nothing gets past you," Cole remarked.

"Where on earth did you get a baby at?" Sis. Gladys asked.

"It was our bargain of the day at the market," Cole replied.

Sis. Gladys was defensive, "It was a simple question."

"We're baby-sitting," Monique informed her.

"Uh, huh." Sis. Gladys wasn't buying the baby-sitting story. Fortunately, for Cole, another knock at the door interrupted.

Opening the door, Cole found a smiling Yossi.

"House call!" Yossi entered the ever crowded hotel room with a small medical bag.

"Dr. Peer, this is Sis. Gladys," Cole said as way of introduction.

"A doctor? Who's sick?" Sis. Gladys asked.

"Well, we didn't want to say anything but the parents of the baby have a really bad virus and the doctor here is going to make sure the baby isn't contagious," Cole explained.

"Contagious?" Worry crept into Sis. Gladys' voice.

Yossi caught the cue from Cole. "I'm afraid so. Very contagious. Hopefully, I won't have to quarantine anyone so they can catch the flight home."

"Maybe I should return to my room. I can show you the scarf some other time." Sis. Gladys was already heading for the door.

"Maybe that's best," Cole agreed.

"I'll call you later," Monique added as the door slammed shut.

"Who was that?" Yossi asked.

"Never mind. Just be glad you aren't flying home with her," Cole stated.

"Shall we examine the child?" Yossi suggested.

Yossi wanted to make sure the child had been taken care of and that there was no hidden ailments that needed attention. As it turned out the child was in remarkable shape.

"That's a blessing," Monique said after Yossi rendered his verdict.

Yossi could tell from that stare in Monique's eyes that Monique was setting herself up for a fall.

"Don't get to attached," he gently warned.

Monique played the innocent, "What do you mean?"

"I mean, you can't keep her," Yossi said.

"What if …" Monique looked at Cole.

Cole intervened, "What if we decided we wanted too?"

"It can't happen. You're American. The baby is Israeli which means she's Jewish and you're not. The government will never approve of such an arrangement. It would create a political uproar," Yossi explained.

"What will happen to her then?" Cole asked.

"Will Lady Marina get her back?" Monique asked.

"Right now, Lady Marina is worried about learning to walk again and staying out of prison. I think she'll be glad Katrina is some place safe and away from her," Yossi replied.

"And where is safe?" Monique wondered.

"I'm working on it," Yossi stated.

Monique retired that evening full of anxiety with little Katrina resting on a small mattress the hotel scrounged up for their use. Though she was worn-out from the day's rollercoaster of events, Monique was too wound up to fall asleep.

She looked over at Cole where the sounds of snoring were flowing freely. Apparently, he had no problem succumbing to exhaustion. It was all right, he'd earned the rest.

Monique caught herself glancing over at Katrina a half dozen times before she told herself she needed to stop. Babies were prone to letting the world know when they were in need.

Staring up at the ceiling, she started listing the reasons she should fight to keep Katrina. Then she quickly reversed herself and began counting the number of reasons backing Yossi's assessment.

Fighting for Katrina was a losing cause. It would drain Cole and her emotionally not to mention the financial aspects which they could least afford right now. They hadn't really discussed the finances, but Monique knew their bank account well enough to realize that even if they kept Katrina without a fight, an extra mouth to feed and clothe was an extra burden they hadn't calculated on.

Somewhere between running figures in her head and imagining what the conversation would be like between her and Cole in the morning, Monique drifted off to sleep. She wasn't aware that she was asleep until she found herself standing back in Caesarea.

"Ah, I see, you've managed to find your way back to us," Phillip said with a sly smile standing in the doorway to his home. He looked no different from how Monique remembered from the last time she saw him.

"Yes, I guess so," Monique answered looking around to gather her bearings.

"Is all well with you?" Phillip asked.

"There's a lot going on," Monique admitted.

"I see. You'll be looking for answers then," Phillip stated.

"Aren't we always looking for answers?" Monique replied.

"Yes, I suppose we are. Won't you come inside? You're always welcomed here. There's another inside but maybe you'll find the answer you need. Come." Phillip motioned for her to follow him through the doorway.

As Monique filed through the doorway, she was sucked into a darkness that was without form or void. She felt herself standing on terra nova but couldn't make out any other recognizable shape.

"You hurt," the Fourth Sister said.

"No, I am fine," Monique replied defensively.

"You're afraid of losing the desire in your grasp," the Fourth Sister told her.

"Ok, maybe, I'm a little apprehensive," Monique admitted.

"Let the child go to one who is in greater need, to one that will love her," the Fourth Sister instructed.

"What's that suppose to mean? Who is in greater need than me, or Katrina for that matter?" Monique questioned.

"Sometimes an act of charity leads us on a path hidden from view. Sometimes, charity is the key for your path to be unveiled. Let the child go," the Fourth Sister said in a fading voice.

Before Monique could respond, she found herself staring up at the ceiling of the hotel room. She glanced over at Katrina who was still asleep. She started to slide up in the bed only to feel Cole sitting up as well. She reached over and turned on the light.

"Sorry, I didn't mean to wake you," Cole said.

"I couldn't sleep. Not really, anyway," Monique told him.

"I just had the most bizarre dream," Cole said causing Monique to jerk her head his way.

"So did I," she replied.

"Mine had to be more bizarre. I was in this darkened house. I had followed this weird looking guy in. And this voice said ..."

Monique interrupted, "Let me guess, charity is the key for your *path to be unveiled*?"

Cole was astonished, "No way."

"Way," Monique confirmed.

The pair sat in silence for several minutes contemplating their thoughts until baby Katrina's cry snapped them back to their present day reality.

.   .   .   .

Yossi sat on a park bench near his flat. It was late and he was tired but he was enjoying the breeze flowing in from the ocean. Besides, he wasn't in the mood to go inside just yet.

He watched as children chased each other down the sidewalk. One stopped long enough to pull a homemade firework from his pocket, light it then toss it up against the wall of a nearby housing unit and walk away like he'd done nothing. The resounding *boom* shattered the calm.

A couple Arab's in their twenties drove by in a car with the windows down and had their stereo playing some sort of rap that Yossi wasn't familiar with and wouldn't have been into anyway. He found it funny to think that these kids thought they were gangsta cool when in fact they didn't have a clue.

A man walking his dog nodded to Yossi as he passed on by. Yossi reached into his pocket for his cellphone.

"I thought you might call," Desica said.

"You did? Why's that?" Yossi asked.

"You seem like the type," she responded.

"What type is that?" Yossi wasn't sure how to take the comment.

"The type I give my number too and who uses it," she replied.

"Is there any chance we can see each other tomorrow?" Yossi suggested.

"Just us or is this a group thing like last time?" Desica wondered.

"Just us. I promise."

"How about dinner tomorrow?" Desica suggested.

"You have a place in mind?" Yossi asked.

"Some place simple. How about Mike's?"

Yossi knew the place. He'd gone there on several occasions to watch sports matches being broadcast from the States.

"That works. Say, 9 o'clock?"

"See you then," Desica said.

Yossi paused for a second and smiled. He didn't know why Desica always seemed to make him smile but he was glad. He picked up the phone and dialed another number and waited for Adi to answer on the other end.

"You and Elain stay home tomorrow. No questions, just trust me on this. Whatever you got to do, stay home. I should be over in the morning at some point. See you then."

Yossi hung up and looked up at the moon. It was a beautiful night indeed.

CHAPTER 15: Uplifts & Let Downs

Yossi paused outside the hotel room door, hesitating out of a sense of dread. He wiped his palms on the side of his pants.

"This is their room?" David asked. The pair had just finished hatching a plan over morning coffee.

Yossi ignored the question and knocked on the door. Cole opened it seconds later and the pair, who was expected, entered a room that by now had the mixed aromas of dirty diapers, formula, cologne and perfume. Monique picked up Katrina and held her tight. She knew what the presence of Yossi signified.

"This is my friend, David Landsberg. Let's just say he's connected and leave it at that," Yossi said.

"I suppose now, you want to take Katrina?" Monique tried to keep her lip from quivering.

"I'm afraid it's time," Yossi informed her.

"But, we thought it might be easier on you if you saw where the baby, was going," David interjected.

"That way, you'll know she has a good home. It might help later," Yossi added.

The group gathered up Katrina's items and crammed them into David's vehicle. Somehow, they all managed to squeeze in with barely enough room to twitch a muscle.

Yossi introduced the Tarkington's to Adi and Elain who had spent the morning pacing their flat. Yossi's phone call after meeting David had made them simultaneously anxious and apprehensive. It wasn't the way they conceived of their wishes being granted but in their hearts they were grateful for however it transpired. Still, they knew those hopes could be dashed at the whim of the Tarkington's.

There was a tense silence as Monique held on to Katrina while looking the new couple and their flat over as though to give them both a seal of approval. Cole who was carrying most of the baby's things, finally, broke the ice.

"Here. You'll find diapers and formula in this bag. I'm afraid the clothes she has on is all she has. We didn't have time to buy new ones yet."

"That's ok. We'll go shopping for her this afternoon." Adi took the items.

"Can I hold her?" Elain asked.

Monique stood in silence, not so much out of reluctance as indecision. Recalling the dream from the night before, she glanced over at Cole.

"Mo, it's time."

Monique looked at Cole, "Sometimes you have to give it up, right?"

"What?" Elain asked.

"It's nothing." Monique gently handed the baby over to Elain.

"Her name is Katrina," Monique told her.

"That's a pretty name," Elain said.

Cole reached over and put his arm around Monique who clearly needed the hug.

David pulled out his card and handed it to Adi. "Come by my office next Tuesday. There will be official adoption papers ready for you to sign."

"How did you arrange this? And so quickly?" Adi inquired.

"Politics is a game of back scratching and someone I knew had a big itch," David explained.

"I want to thank you. You have no … well, this means so much to us," Elain told the Tarkington's.

"Yes, you two are welcomed in our home any time," Adi said.

"Thank you." Cole watched as Monique turned and headed for the door.

There was one more stop on Yossi's agenda. The ride was silent and everyone was quietly concerned about Monique who stared out of the window at passing pedestrians.

Monique wasn't sure she could take any more ups and downs on this trip. Right now, the way she felt, she only wanted to return to her home in St. Clair, Indiana and never leave town again. She never imagined feeling this way but sanctuary was what her soul sought at the moment.

Cole knew better than to say anything. There would be a time and place for his support but right now, he knew Monique had to work through her own emotions first. Anything else was bound to be just salt poured on the wound.

"Maybe we should just go back to the hotel," Cole suggested.

"No, I don't think so. Trust me. This is one surprise you don't want to miss." Yossi told them.

"I'm not sure I can survive any more surprises," Monique said out loud to no one in particular.

"Monique. The day isn't over," Yossi said attempting to pick up her spirits.

Monique looked at him without a flinch, "That's what I'm afraid of."

David turned the car into the driveway of the underground garage of the famous Opera Sea Tower which was located about a block from the ocean and with its distinctive terrace look, was one of the most famous designs in the Tel Aviv skyline.

A security guard stopped the car to inspect it. David whipped out his identification and the guard motioned them on through the gate. David drove to a spot on the far end of the garage where another vehicle was parked in a reserved location. Stopping the vehicle, David put it in park but left the engine running.

"This is where everyone gets out," David said.

As they stretched their legs, the door to the car in the reserved space opened and out stepped the aide from the Interior Ministry. He was with Aleta whom he gently led by the hand.

"Thanks for coming on short notice," David said.

"If we can pull this off, it will be well worth the effort," the aide replied.

"What's he talking about?" Monique looked at Cole for an answer but he was busy being dumbfounded by the sight of Aleta who, with two fingers stuck in her mouth, was staring back with a shy look of recognition.

"Yossi?" Monique asked.

"Well …" Yossi never got a chance to complete his answer as Aleta walked over on her own to Cole who scooped her up.

"This is Aleta. The little girl I told you about from the other night," Cole explained. "I don't understand. What is this?"

"Well, with both parents dead, the child, Aleta, is scheduled to be disposed of by the Interior Ministry," the aide said.

"Disposed of?" Monique said horrified.

"That is the wrong word. She'll be deported back to Ethiopia," David explained.

"She has relatives there?" Cole asked.

"None that we can tell or at least none that want to claim her," the aide informed them.

Yossi spoke up, "So, David and I devised this little get together to see if maybe …."

"We help the ministry avoid returning a child to Ethiopia to be orphaned in return for juggling the paperwork for Katrina so that Adi and Elain can keep her," David told them.

"Saves all parties concerned any embarrassment should word leak out," the aide explained.

"Aleta this is Monique," Cole told the child.

"I know it is sudden and it is a bit of a snap decision especially when considering the long term implications, but what do you say? Instead of Katrina, think you can give this child a home?" Yossi asked.

Cole and Monique locked eyes. Monique looked at the child and then back at the Cole.

"What are you thinking?" she asked Cole.

"The child does need a home," he replied.

Monique reached out and took the child from Cole. Aleta didn't squirm or fuss but instead started playing with Monique's hair.

"If you agree, we'll have the paperwork prepared and in a month, I'll fly her over myself," David explained.

"This is ok with the American government?" Cole asked.

"Normally, no. But like I said before, politics is a game of back scratching," David answered.

The aide chimed in, "We made a call."

"Don't fool yourself, it won't be easy. But you will be literally saving a child," Yossi told them.

"How can I say 'no' to that?" Monique responded.

"You heard the lady. Set it in motion." It felt so right what they were doing that Cole couldn't imagine it being wrong.

Monique looked at Aleta, "I hope you like boys because you're going to be a big surprise to one young fellow back in the States."

.   .   .   .

"You look tired," Desica noted as she slid onto the outdoor wooden bench at Mike's Place. The establishment was a hub for expats especially if you wanted to see a live Blue's band or catch a major sports event originating outside Israel. Very few Israeli's actually visited Mike's and most of the staff were olim from Europe or the U.S as was the waitress who took their order.

"Yeah, well, it's been a long, tiring day," Yossi replied without delving into details.

"I've noticed that about you," Desica said.

"What?" Yossi asked.

"You always seem to have long, stressful days," Desica replied.

"Is that a bad thing?"

"Yes."

"Why is that?"

Desica shrugged her shoulders. "I don't know. There is the stock answer that life is short. You have to stop and smell the roses, that sort of thing."

"Ok, those are the stock answers. What is *your* reason?" Yossi pressed.

"It's boring," she replied.

"Boring?"

"Boring. You know when I first saw you in that café in Jerusalem, I thought to myself, now here is a guy who needs a little excitement in his life. He just needs a little incentive, mainly me, to find it. But ever since then, you're always in deep thought, in the middle of a crisis of some sort, or just stressed out."

"And that is a turn off?" Yossi asked.

"I thought you were cute and that we'd have fun so yeah, it's a turn off," Desica confirmed.

"Up until about 30 seconds ago, I really liked you," Yossi observed.

"I know. That's why I'm saying this now. I want to prevent hurt before it happens."

"How sweet of you," Yossi's voice had turned biting and sarcastic.

"Let me tell you about my boring day. I was in an operating room doing my best to make sure a friend kept

the use of her legs. I helped a couple people arrange homes
for two children that would otherwise be dumped onto the
street somewhere. Now, I am sorry if none of that sounds
fun enough for you but while stressful, it has been a pretty
satisfying day up until now." It was all Yossi could do to
keep from shouting.

Desica felt put off. She hadn't expected Yossi to react
this harshly. "I'm sorry. I didn't know."

"How could you? You never asked." There was a pause
as the two looked directly in each other's eyes.

"I tell you what, Desica, while it has been a pleasure
meeting you, maybe it'd be best if you'd just go like you
were planning to do in the first place," Yossi suggested.

She could've asked how he knew that her original
intention was to get up and leave as soon as this
conversation ended but she supposed it didn't matter in the
end. The result was the same.

Desica stood up from the table and looked down at Yossi
who didn't return the parting glance. The waitress, who'd
been in the process of stopping at the table to make sure
everything was fine, paused in her tracks, even back
tracking two or three steps to avoid being caught in any
exploding fireworks.

Desica kept her tone low and her voice calm, "I'm sorry. But if you ever want to cut loose, feel free to give me a call. You have the number."

Yossi refused to let his eyes follow her as she left Mike's Place and headed down the boardwalk. As the waitress finally made her approach, he said, "Guess you'd better bring me a bill."

Yossi was standing on the beach. The moonlight was catching the foam of the waves just right and they showed up in the night almost like they were part of a painting.

Somewhere out there, if he kept going straight, Yossi would find home. Somewhere, but only the outgoing tide would be able to tell him how far it was and how to reach it.

Yossi held his watch up to the moonlight then reached for his cell.

"Hey, Mike! How is life among the stars man? Hey, you know that job you'd emailed me about? Think you could email me specifics?" The time for a change had come.

. . . .

Guy was waiting patiently on the Yafo docks in front of the same warehouse he and Lady Marina had made their deal several nights ago. He was glad that she had survived her mishap. The information she had provided him would help seal Yuri's fate.

Dr. Peer seemed to be genuinely looking out for her. In Lady Marina's position, she was lucky she had a friendly doctor overseeing her case. Dr. Peer seemed to think it would take several months before Lady Marina would regain a semblance of her life back but at least the bottom line was she was going to make it.

Guy's interest perked up with the faint appearance of headlights in the distance. He reached behind him and gave three short raps on the warehouse door.

The lights raced toward him and the Mercedes they belonged too quickly screeched to a halt a few feet from the place where Guy was standing. Like any other night when business was being transacted, it was just Guy and the customer he was expecting.

Yuri exited from the driver's seat leaving the lights on and the engine running. Angry at having been dragged away from dinner with his family this time of the evening, he demanded, "What is this all about, Guy?"

"Someone hasn't been following orders. I thought you had better see this for yourself before I did anything," Guy explained.

"What do you mean?" Yuri wanted to know.

Guy motioned toward the warehouse, "Open it up yourself."

Yuri reached for his key chain, stuck it into the lock on the doors, and then with a turn of the wrist, flung them open.

"What?" Yuri yelled as a half dozen lights hit him and a squad of men, armed with automatic weapons pointed at his face, began yelling for him to put his hands up. He knew he had nowhere to run.

In the middle of the men was the girl who'd been left behind the night Guy and Lady Marina had picked up their human cargo. Guy had rescued her later but led Yuri to believe she had been dumped out at sea as ordered.

Now the woman, facing the scourge who had destroyed her life and nearly killed her, walked up to Yuri with the muscles in her face twitching from the anger she felt.

"You're supposed to be dead," a startled Yuri uttered as the officers began cuffing him. The woman's reply was a wad of spittle to the face.

"I don't think she approved of your original plan, Yuri," Guy said.

"You'll pay for this. You hear me? I will personally make sure you suffer for this," Yuri threatened as Guy motioned for his unit to take the prisoner away.

Guy looked at the woman who was feeling some measure of satisfaction. "They always make promises they can't keep. Listen, are you hungry? I know this great pizza place. You like pizza? How about I drive?"

CHAPTER 16: Six Months Later

"How is the pizza?" Guy asked.

"As good as I remembered." Lady Marina caught a piece of cheese that was hanging from her mouth and let out a chuckle.

"One last piece for the road," Guy informed her.

Lady Marina was caught off-guard, "What do you mean?"

Guy pushed an envelope at her from across the table. She wiped her hands of pizza grease and cautiously opened it up. Her eyes grew wide which was more expression than she was use to publicly indicating. She retrieved a passport from inside and held it up as though further confirmation was still needed.

"That's right. You're going home. Back to the Ukraine," Guy told her.

"When?" Lady Marina asked.

"Tonight."

"I want to hug you," Lady Marina gleefully confessed.

"Resist the temptation. This is the least I can do. Inside the envelope you'll find a bank account number for you to access when you get to Kiev," Guy explained.

"I don't know how to thank you," Lady Marina admitted.

Guy responded, "It's the least I can do. You might have to learn to adjust to those Ukrainian winters though."

"True, it has been awhile."

"Oh, there is one more thing." Guy reached for his phone, did a quick scroll then hit a contact number. A second later Lady Marina's ringtone sounded. After glancing at the phone, she looked up suspiciously at Guy, then opened the text message he had sent her.

The message contained a video link. She couldn't know she'd feel such a wave a joy from hitting the play button. There in a short one minute video was Katrina with Elain and Adi. The whole family was sending their greetings that ended with a close-up of Katrina.

"They gave it to Yossi who sent it to me and now me to you," Guy explained. "A little memento to take with you back to the Ukraine."

"Thank you," Lady Marina softly said.

Guy told her, "A car is waiting for you outside to take you to pack your things and go to the airport."

Clutching the phone as though it was the most precious of possessions, Lady Marina grabbed the cane she was still having to use to get around with, stood, and with a goodbye nod to Guy turned for the door.

Guy watched her leave and climb into a car that whisked her away. As he left the cash on the table for the bill, he played the video on his phone again. The smile on Katrina's face was big and joyful. The kid was going to have a chance after all. As he stood up, he hit the delete button.

Our view of The Assignment

According to Gods Word, Jesus Christ will NOT return until the Gospel is preached to all the world as a witness to all nations. Every nation, tribe, people and language will be represented in the blood-washed Church of Jesus Christ. We believe it should be a birth right for every person to hear the Gospel at least one time in their life.

Our mission; One Chance for Every Person!

Box 8700, Fresno, CA 93747, USA

Toll Free (800) 745 1332, Fax (866) 888 0572, e-mail: JCl@joshuacampaign.com

www.joshuacampaign.com

www.missionsoneeleven.com

www.theassignmentshow.tv

www.ingramcontent.com/pod-product-compliance
Lightning Source LLC
Chambersburg PA
CBHW070659180626
46817CB00006B/2443